Was it a just a kiss?

Jamie wasn't sure because it felt more like their mouths had just had hot, sweaty sex.

"Wow." Daisy sat back, touching her lips, her eyes wide in disbelief.

"Between here and there, you need to decide if you want me to come up."

"I do?"

"Yes."

They walked out the door, greeted by the cool Chicago evening. Daisy paused beside the bike, looking up at him with an intoxicating mixture of wonder and wantonness. "What will happen if you come up?"

He leaned down and kissed her softly, exhibiting way more control than he had any right to show. "Dessert."

"Oh. Well, there's lots of that. Pie, chocolate torte, lemon meringue. What would you like?"

"You."

Dear Reader,

I love contradictions. Things like opposites attract, cheering for the underdog, wanting to get down and dirty in a boxing ring...hmm, is that a contradiction or a scene from the book?

Either way, when I pitched a story about a bakery and a boxing club, I wasn't sure it was going to fly. But it did—I guess boxing and baking do mix—and *Sweet Seduction* was born. The story features the lovely Daisy and the hotter-than-hell Jamie, a lawyer and private boxing club owner who thinks Daisy is even tastier than her delicious baked goods, which he adores in a finger-licking, groaning sort of orgasmic way.

While that might not be my exact experience with baking, it's pretty damn close. My favorite thing is the cinnamon bun—thanks to my mom who makes the best cinnamon buns ever. To this day, the smell of warm, fresh bread slathered in butter, cinnamon and brown sugar gooeyness is synonymous with comfort and home, just as it is for Daisy.

As for the boxing? Besides the fact that ripped, shirtless guys duking it out is hot, growing up with three older brothers and a mother who only knows one haircut—a boy cut (aka pixie cut)—meant that when I tagged along to boxing practice with my brothers, their coaches asked why their "little brother" didn't join in. So I did.

I hope you enjoy *Sweet Seduction* and stay tuned for the second book in the series, *Big Sky Seduction*, featuring Daisy's best friend Gloria.

Happy reading!

Daire St. Denis

Daire St. Denis

Sweet Seduction

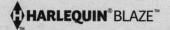

HARLEQUIN® BLAZE™

Recycling programs
for this product may
not exist in your area.

ISBN-13: 978-0-373-79889-6

Sweet Seduction

Printed in U.S.A.

New York Times and *USA TODAY* bestselling author **Daire St. Denis** is an adventure seeker, an ancient history addict, a seasonal hermit and a wine lover. She calls the Canadian Rockies home and has the best job ever: writing smoking-hot contemporary romance where the pages are steeped in sensuality and there's always a dash of the unexpected. Find out more about Daire and subscribe to her newsletter at dairestdenis.com.

For Lady Laine, the best baker I know.

_1_

DAISY SINCLAIR'S PHONE came alive on her desk, jumping and jiving to "Candy" by Foxy Brown. She'd been so absorbed in entering information into Accounts Payable that the sudden noise startled her silly.

"What's up?" Daisy said aloud, picking up the device and checking the message on the screen. It was the reminder she'd set four weeks ago. Four _hellish_ weeks ago. And now, four weeks later, the reminder was telling her it was _time_. Time to face the music. Time to see whether the torture she'd put herself through had all been worth it.

After nudging the scale out from beneath her desk, Daisy tiptoed to her office door and shut it. Then she gave herself a once-over in the full-length mirror on the back of the door. There was a streak of flour on her cheek that she rubbed off with the back of her hand before her gaze dropped. Hmm. The apron she wore made her look boxy.

She untied it and slipped it off.

Unfortunately, the well-worn jeans and loose cotton blouse weren't much better, so she stripped those off, too, dropping them in a pile by the door.

There. Now she could see what was what. She'd avoided the full-length mirror for four weeks for just this purpose.

The celebrity gala that her mother had managed to get her a ticket to was on Saturday, only five days away, and she was determined to look her best in her fabulous new red dress—hence the month of hell she'd endured. Daisy swiveled in front of the mirror, eyes narrowed, searching her figure for the changes that had to be there.

Generous hips.

She turned to check out her butt.

Round ass.

Standing in profile, she cupped a hand under her breasts.

Biggish boobs.

Daisy sighed. She looked *exactly* the same.

Healthy. Nana Sin's voice was so clear it was as if her grandmother was standing right beside her, smiling, holding a tray of freshly baked caramel-nut cookies.

Stubborn cow was the *endearment* Daisy's ex-jerk-of-a-husband had for her. But then, she'd had a few choice names for him, too, over the course of their short marriage. The divorce would have been done with by now if it wasn't for Nana Sin's bakery.

Ahh, the bakery. Daisy closed her eyes and took a deep breath. The cinnamon buns must be fresh out of the oven because the aroma of cinnamon with an overtone of raisins, sweet and sticky with brown-sugar yumminess, was heavy in the air. Heaven. This had to be what Heaven smelled like.

Okay, once this business with the scale was over, she was going to reward herself with a bun. She deserved it.

With a deep breath and then another, she stepped up onto the scale and peered cautiously over the tips of her candy-floss painted toenails.

Daisy blinked.

She blinked again.

No.

She stepped off and checked the setting on the scale.

Yes, it was at zero. She gave it a few good shakes to reset it—or whatever a good shake was supposed to do—and carefully stepped back onto the thing, thinking the lightest of thoughts. An image of impossibly thin phyllo pastry, brushed with melted butter and filled with nuts and honey, came to mind. She envisioned herself sliding the baking sheet out of the oven, the phyllo a golden brown. She could practically taste it, light as a cloud, melting on her tongue, honey trickling sweetly down her throat…

Hmm. Those were probably the wrong kinds of "light" thoughts to be having.

Daisy squinted hard at the number dial on the top of the foul instrument sent from Lucifer himself.

No, no, no, no, no!

How could she have spent four weeks on the Summer Size Diet Plan and not have shed one pound? Not only that, how could she have gained five? It defied sense. It was contrary to reason!

Four weeks of abstaining from tarts and pies.

Four weeks of drooling over sweet breads and butter-frosted cupcakes, only to pass them up.

Four weeks of avoiding cheese buns and chocolate mousse tortes and baklava and angel food cake and whipped cream and apple strudel and…all for nothing?

Daisy paced her office while she contemplated the miserable joke the universe had played on her. It wasn't fair. She'd been a saint, exercising and cutting back and avoiding the baked goods, which was tantamount to pure torture when she owned the flipping bakery. And her bakery wasn't just *any* bakery, but the best damn bakery in Bucktown, the city of Chicago, the state of Illinois—why, maybe even the whole country, for all she knew. Sure, that was hard to prove, but the point was, she'd managed to abstain from some pretty fine friggin' food and the result was a gain of five pounds?

Daisy kicked the scale.

Dammit!

She lifted her foot to massage her stubbed big toe while hopping around on the other. Once the throbbing stopped, she picked up the offending scale and waved it in the air, speaking to whoever might be up there listening. "Do you think this is funny? Do you think you can knock me down? Ha! I'm not some fragile waif, so bring it on, Universe. Come on. I dare you. I can take whatever you dish out."

With the scale poised above her head, its destruction imminent, she watched the door to her office open. A tall, broad and, most importantly, *clothed* man walked in.

He was followed closely by Lizzie, her assistant baker, who ended up bumping into the back of him because he'd stopped to stare—with his mouth hanging open.

"Boss!" Lizzie cried. "What the—"

Her heart went *thrump* and Daisy felt her face turn the shade of maraschino cherry juice.

"Oh." The man—who was so conveniently dressed—just stood and stared.

Daisy tried in vain to cover her bits and pieces with the scale. "Get out!" When the man didn't move, she shouted, "Hello? Out!" She pointed to the door.

Lizzie scampered through the door but the man did not. He stood frozen like the ice-cream cake stashed at the back of her freezer.

"Is something wrong with you?"

He shook his head, not embarrassed in the least— horrible, horrible man! He opened his mouth as if to say something, but then stopped himself and finally ducked out the door. Before Daisy had time to collapse in mortification, the door opened a crack and the guy stuck his head back through. "Break that thing."

"Oh, my God!" She hugged the scale to her chest. "Go away!"

The door shut and Daisy kept the scale close until she reached her pile of clothes. She dropped the scale and then struggled into her jeans before fumbling with the buttons on her blouse. Once dressed, she looked up, catching a glimpse of her haphazard appearance in the mirror. Her cheeks were flushed, making her eyes overly bright. Daisy covered her face, hoping the action would block out what just happened.

No such luck.

There was a tentative knock at the door, and Daisy wrenched it open to find Lizzie standing there looking sheepish.

"Oh, so now you knock?"

"Sorry, I—"

"Why on earth didn't you knock the first time?" Daisy demanded.

"I did," Lizzie explained. "I thought I heard you say 'come in.'" She frowned. "You were saying a bunch of stuff. I didn't catch the last part. Something about bringing a dish out?"

Daisy pressed her fingers to her temples. "That makes no sense."

"I know. But you're always saying stuff that doesn't make sense. I was sure I heard you say 'come in.'" Lizzie tilted her head, thinking. "Or maybe it was 'come on.' Either way."

Daisy collapsed in her chair. "So, who's the guy I indecently exposed myself to?"

Lizzie cleared her throat. "Colin Forsythe." She forced a smile.

The name had Daisy sitting up straight in her chair. "Oh, God. No. Tell me I didn't."

"Mmm, you kind of did."

"As in food critic and columnist from the *Tribune*, Colin Forsythe?"

"That would be the one."

"No." Daisy dropped her head into her hands, the world collapsing around her. She buried her face, hoping she'd get sucked into the black hole created by the implosion of her life.

There was a knock, and Daisy whipped her head around to stare at the door in horror.

"The man himself beckons." Lizzie twiddled her fingers in the direction of the door like an amateur magician.

"Tell him to go away. Tell him I'm Maisy, Daisy's deranged twin sister, and that the real Daisy will be back from vacation next week."

"See?" Lizzie said, pointing at her. "This is what I'm talking about. You say these things sometimes. Then I think you're telling me to come in when really you're doing some weird underwear dance. What were you doing, by the way?"

"Oh, God."

Lizzie reached across the desk and patted Daisy's arm. "You know what? So you traipse around in your office naked-ish. Who cares? You're the boss. Just get out there and pretend like nothing happened. Do it with a smile." She demonstrated an example of a big, fake smile. Not helpful.

It was easy for Lizzie to tell her to face the man with a smile when she wasn't the one who had just been discovered pacing her office in her unmentionables. Daisy plucked her blouse from her chest for a quick peek to remind herself exactly which unmentionables she was wearing. Well, at least it was her new Victoria's Secret satin set. So, her undies were nice; that was hardly a consolation.

"Ms. Sinclair?"

She looked up at the man standing in the doorway to her office. Yes, he was Colin Forsythe all right. His wavy brown hair might have been a bit longer than in the picture beside his column, but he had the same square jaw, the same nose—though in person it was a little crooked—and the same full lips. While he was recognizable, his byline picture did not do him justice. In that picture he came off as stern, albeit in a well-coiffed, intellectual sort of way. Actually, his picture made him look snooty. In person? Wow. He looked anything but. His eyes sparkled with irreverence, his lips turned up at one side as if he was trying to keep a sinful smile in check, and he was just…bigger. More like a professional athlete than a distinguished foodie.

His eyebrows rose under her appraisal. "Do I pass?"

Daisy cringed. Good-looking. Big ego. No surprise. Obviously, he was going to make this impossible for her. But he was Colin Forsythe, and she'd been anticipating this interview ever since taking over Nana Sin's bakery three years ago. Of course he had to show up today of all days. That was just her luck. Someone, somewhere had a warped sense of humor where she was concerned. Daisy paused, cocking her head. Weird. Sometimes she was sure she could hear her grandmother chuckling, as though she was standing right behind her.

"Is everything okay?"

She sent an incredulous look at the much too tall, far too self-assured man standing in her doorway. "Are you kidding me?"

"Please don't be embarrassed."

"Can we pretend, for my sake, that we're meeting for the first time, right now? That you didn't just…" Daisy paused to take a deep, composing breath. She stood, shoulders back. "Hello, Mr. Forsythe." She walked around her desk, hand outstretched. "I'm Daisy Sinclair. Welcome to Nana Sin's."

He rubbed his jaw as if trying to massage his face into a serious expression. It didn't work. When she was close enough, he took her hand and shook it firmly. She thought he might take the opportunity to say something crass, but all he said was, "It's Colin."

"Colin." She set her lips in a grim line and sauntered past, head held high. At the door she turned. "Shall we?"

"Shall we what?"

Daisy rolled her eyes. "The bakery." She indicated the kitchen with the motion of her head. "Aren't you here to see the bakery?"

In one step Colin was beside her, looking down at her. Damn, the man was tall. Not fair. And what the hell was he doing, blasting her with that sinful smile of his?

"I've already seen everything." He grinned.

She groaned.

His gaze held hers for a second before flicking toward the front of the building. "I'm talking about the bakery. I spent the last half hour in the front, interviewing customers and your staff."

"You did?"

"Yes. Customers here all ask for you. By name."

With a shrug, Daisy said, "The bakery's been here a long time. People are loyal."

"Only when they have a reason to be."

"I suppose…"

He came closer, spoke more softly. "What I'd really like is a taste."

The way he looked at her made Daisy think he wanted to taste *her*. Of all the ridiculous, embarrassing, appealing ideas she'd ever had, this one took the cake. With a huff, she marched past him into the kitchen, her jaw clamped shut, ignoring the deep rumbling sound of his chuckle. Wicked, wicked man. When she caught sight of Lizzie punching some dough, she snapped. "Lizzie, it's the morning rush. Julia can't handle the store alone."

"But the dough…"

"I'll take care of it."

Lizzie scurried out through the double doors to the front, leaving Daisy with the dough and Colin Forsythe. After donning one of the extremely unattractive hair nets—she was beyond caring how she looked—and thoroughly washing her hands, she took over Lizzie's job. Punching dough was exactly what she needed right now.

"You're really letting that dough have it."

"Some doughs need a gentle touch. Others need a good, hard spanking." Daisy regretted the words the second they came out of her mouth. "Please don't quote me there."

"Shame. It's a good quote." Colin said, coughing to cover up a laugh. "I thought bakeries did all the baking in the early hours."

Daisy scratched an itchy spot on her chin with her shoulder and then gave the dough another punch, getting less satisfaction than normal from the warm, airy flour as it enclosed her fist and the smell of yeast that always accompanied the task. At the very least, his question was professional, so Daisy answered, hoping her voice sounded more composed than she felt. "It's one of the reasons we're so popular. We offer fresh baking all day long, featuring different bestsellers every day of the week. Tuesdays are cinnamon-bun days. These should be ready for lunch, and we'll do another batch for the after-work crowd."

"You're always this busy?"

"Always."

"How many people do you have working here?"

"Two full-time girls at the counter, although Chrissy's sick today, and Lizzie and Bruce help me in the kitchen. Then I've got five part-timers for evenings and weekends." It was then that Daisy noticed Colin Forsythe had no pen. No paper. He wasn't even recording this. She frowned. "You're not taking any of this down?"

He tapped the side of his head. "It's all up here. Don't you worry."

After finishing with the huge bowl, Daisy covered it with a clean, damp cloth and placed it in the warmer to rise. Then she started on the next. She found it much easier to talk to Colin when she didn't have to look at him and her hands were busy, keeping her mind focused on something other than the fact that he'd seen more of her than any man had in a *very* long time.

Colin pulled up a stool and sat down, watching her work. "How do you keep up with it?"

"It's easy." She glanced up. "I love it. Spending my time here isn't work. And the staff—well, we're like one big family." The only person missing from that family was Nana. God, how she missed her.

"The sign on the door says Nana Sin's been around for fifty years. How did you acquire it?"

"It was my grandmother's. After she died, I inherited it." And it did belong to her, no matter what Alan's lawyer said. Daisy glanced down. Seeing her ex's face superimposed on the bowl of dough, she gave the lump a good hard whack.

"How long have you worked here?"

"I can't really say. I've basically spent most of my life here." She glanced around the big kitchen. Though she'd made some updates since taking over three years ago, the kitchen still evoked the same memories. It didn't matter that it looked different than it did when she was growing up. The smell was the same. Yeast, brown sugar, cinnamon, baked butter—it was synonymous with her grandmother, synonymous with safety and security and home.

"Tell me, Daisy…may I call you Daisy?"

"I think we're past formalities."

Colin chuckled deep inside that stupidly big chest of his. "When do I get to sample something?"

She blinked at him. A strange heat crept up the inside of her ribcage to settle at the base of her throat. Did he intend to sound suggestive? Because all Daisy could think about was Colin Forsythe sampling something much more… intimate than cinnamon buns. Her mouth and bare skin, for example.

Dammit, Daisy! Just because he saw you in your hot pink undies does not make him hot for you. Besides, he's clearly an ass. Isn't one ass in your lifetime enough?

The thought made her simultaneously hot and cold.

Colin grinned as if he knew exactly what she was thinking and motioned to a half dozen fresh buns sitting on cooling racks.

"Oh. Of course." When he went to grab a bun, she slapped his hand, an automatic reaction, but one that felt way too familiar. She cleared her throat. "Not those. They're for Johnny." Daisy grabbed a plate from the cupboard and separated a bun from the others cooling. When she passed him the plate, she made certain their fingers did not come in contact.

No more touching. No more thoughts of touching.

Colin leaned over the plate and took a deep breath. His brows drew together, and a look of bliss came over him. It *almost* redeemed him in Daisy's eyes.

Almost.

He lifted the bun and held it in front of his face before taking a big bite. His brows lifted and then dropped.

"Mmm." He turned to her, rapture written in the gleam of his eyes. He slowly took another bite. And then another. After his fourth—not that Daisy was counting—he said with a still partially full mouth, "Wow. So good."

"Thank you."

He finished chewing and then turned the plate in his hand, inspecting the last bite. "It's perfect. You know that, right? The outside is crisp, the inside soft. They're sweet and sticky, but the sweetness is balanced with the freshness of the bread." He cocked his head to the side and asked, "Aren't you having some?"

Daisy pressed her lips together. The buns were her all-time favorite, and witnessing Colin's unrestrained enthusiasm—the groans, the finger licking, the orgasmic look on his face—evoked an aberrant longing that made it hard to breathe.

Orgasmic look? Where the hell did that thought come from? Sheesh!

"Here, have some of mine." Colin held out the remaining bite for her.

Daisy backed away because the pull to lean forward and take the bite—with her mouth, right from his hand—was overpowering. "No, thanks," she said, staring at his fingers, a vivid image of herself licking them ricocheting inside her head.

"You don't eat your own baking?"

"Oh, yeah. All the time. Just not today."

He narrowed his eyes. Under his scrutiny, Daisy felt like the shy, insecure kid she'd once been, desperate to please.

"Please tell me that *you*, of all people, are not on a diet."

"What if I am?" Daisy asked defensively.

"I'd say stop." He leaned back, crossed his arms on his broad chest and let his eyes wander over her body.

Daisy blew out air through pursed lips. "Whatever." She

waved dismissively at him. "Can we get back to talking about Nana Sin's—"

"Can I tell you what I see?"

"It's really none of your—"

He got up, and his swift approach made Daisy forget what she was about to say. With him standing so close, she was forced to look up at him, *way* up at him. His presence overwhelmed her, as did his cologne. What was it? Something masculine. Something that contrasted with the sweet and savory aromas ever-present in the bakery. Something that had her blood pressure rising in direct proportion to each and every incredible inch he towered over her.

"You're gorgeous," he said matter-of-factly.

"You mean big-boned."

"No. That is not what I mean."

Daisy tried to shrug away from this presumptuous man, but for each step she backed away, he took one to close the distance. She hoped to sound light and breezy when she said, "If I'm not big-boned, that only leaves me with one other descriptor."

"Yes." His voice dropped an octave as his eyelids lowered to half-mast. "Curvy."

"You mean plump."

"I mean perfect."

Oh, my God. Did his eyes just drop to her boobs? "This is not appropriate."

"Probably not. Though neither is greeting me in smokin' hot underwear."

She covered her face, and he pulled her hands away, dropping his head toward her. "But that's not the best part." For a startling moment, Daisy thought Colin Forsythe was going to kiss her. More surprising, Daisy *hoped* he would. Oh, good lord. There was something wrong with her!

Colin didn't kiss her, however. Oh, no. What he did was

almost more intimate in Daisy's estimation. He shut his eyes and took in a long, slow, deep breath. His smile grew as leisurely as his exhalation.

"Vanilla, orange zest, cinnamon…" He paused to inhale even more deeply right by Daisy's cheek. "And rosemary. That last one is unexpected, but very nice."

Daisy stared at him. At his lips, more specifically. Her heart pounded like a meat tenderizer whacking away in her chest. She'd made rosemary and orange crisps early that morning. How on earth had he detected that? Was it possible that for the first time in her life, she'd met a person with a sense of smell as powerful as her own?

No, it couldn't be.

But even more unbelievable was the fact that this much too tall, far too arrogant, nosy man was licking his lips like the next thing he wanted to sample was Daisy herself.

2

"HERE'S TO NANA SIN'S."

"Thanks, Glo." Daisy raised her glass and clinked it against her best friend's.

"Don't thank me. I've been waiting for a reason to come to Le Beau Monde ever since it opened. Your recent celebrity status is the perfect excuse. Tonight's on me, by the way."

Daisy blushed. Actually, she'd been blushing for three days straight, ever since Colin Forsythe's article—not just a review, but a half-page feature—had appeared in the *Tribune*.

Her blush became a full-body flush when Gloria quoted a line from the review. "'Daisy Sinclair, who is as sinfully delicious and entertaining as the bakery itself, runs Nana Sin's like it is her own kitchen, creating a cozy, familiar atmosphere with some of the finest pastries I've ever encountered.' Good lord, Daise, it's like the guy's smitten with you or something."

"Yeah, well…" She hadn't told Gloria about the underwear debacle or the outright flirting that ensued. Gloria would only read more into the encounter than there was. Plus, Daisy didn't want to jinx things for Saturday's date.

Not that she believed in jinxes. She mostly didn't. But it'd been a long time since her last date, and Daisy figured it was better to play it safe and keep it on the down low for now.

God! She had a date with Colin Forsythe. How on earth did that happen? Daisy replayed the scene over in her mind while nodding absently as Gloria gave her typical monologue, assessing the decor of the restaurant—hazards of being an interior designer and stager.

"Are you listening?" Gloria asked.

"Yep."

"Why are your eyes closed?"

Daisy's eyes popped open. "Sorry. Go on. You were saying something about paisley."

Once Gloria started in on the upholstery again, Daisy went back to her daydream. She remembered Colin checking his watch and swearing under his breath because it was later than he'd thought. When she went to shake his hand goodbye, he held hers instead of shaking it.

What are you doing Saturday? Even after replaying that line a bajillion times in her head, Daisy still felt a weird somersault-y thing in her stomach.

When she told him she was going to the Celebrity Hors d'oeuvres Gala, he'd taken her hand, turned it over, kissed the back of her knuckles and asked her if she would do him the honor of accompanying her to the Gala, as he was going, as well.

Seriously.

It was like something out of one of the historical-romance novels she absolutely adored. Sure, he was only playing at being chivalrous, but it had worked. Holy Hannah, had it worked. Even now parts of Daisy's anatomy came alive, parts that had been dormant for too long.

"Why are you smiling?" Gloria asked.

"I'm happy. That's all." Daisy took a sip of her cosmopolitan, hoping to cover up her giddiness and the fact that she hadn't been listening to her friend.

Thankfully the server appeared with their food, giving Daisy an excuse to focus on something other than Colin Forsythe and her friend's much too perceptive appraisal of her strange behavior. She'd spill everything to Gloria after the date.

"Your duck looks delicious," Gloria said, pulling out her cell phone and taking a picture. Then she snapped a few of her own dish.

"What are you doing?"

"Instagram, baby." Gloria showed her the pictures— pretty amazing quality for a cell phone. "People love pictures of food almost as much as they love the real thing."

"Not me. It's the real thing or nothing." Now that Daisy was off the diet wagon, she cheerfully sliced into her candied breast of duck with a garlic-caramel sauce. Placing the food in her mouth, she sat for a minute, savoring the sweet, tender meat.

"What do you think?"

"Mmm." Daisy raised her cloth napkin to her lips. "The French know how to cook."

She took another bite of the duck and then followed it with a forkful of risotto. "Oh, my God!" She covered her mouth in ecstasy. "I think I've just died and gone to heaven. I'm sure I taste lavender in this and maybe… Gloria? Are you okay?"

Her best friend seemed more interested in a table across the restaurant than in her.

"What is it?"

Gloria half stood to get a better look at whatever it was that had caught her attention. "Isn't that him?"

"Who?" Daisy turned to look where her friend was trying to point inconspicuously with her chin.

Across the room, a man sat alone at his table, eyes closed, a pencil poised in his hand, wearing an expression that was so serious it bordered on comical. He'd had his hair cut, but there was no mistaking him.

Colin.

Daisy couldn't swallow. She took a gulp of water to wash the risotto down and then stared. A moment later, as if he could feel her gaze, he opened his eyes and stared right back. Daisy smiled. Then she blushed. Or, she blushed, then smiled. It was hard to tell which came first.

Colin looked away.

"That's him, isn't it? Colin Forsythe?" Gloria whispered.

"Yes."

"Have you thanked him for the review?"

"No, I…" She'd wanted to. In fact, she'd gone as far as picking up the phone two or three hundred times for just that purpose. But every time she did, she'd put it right back down, not wanting to seem too eager, wanting to wait until Saturday to thank him.

"Go thank him."

Of course she should thank him. It only made sense. But for some reason, the risotto she'd swallowed felt like jumping beans in her belly, and her hands had gone cold while her cheeks were about to spontaneously combust. She was being silly. He was *just* a man, and she was *just* a woman— a woman he'd already seen in her undies. No big deal.

Yeah, right.

With a deep breath, Daisy straightened her shoulders, folded her napkin and strolled up to Colin's table, trying to ignore the swarm of bees swirling around in her belly. She was anxious to blurt out her thanks the moment she reached his side but stopped herself when she realized he was still eating with his eyes closed. Actually, *eating* didn't accurately describe what he was doing. He seemed to be rolling the food around in his mouth, letting every single one of his taste buds have a go at whatever was there. He was making noises, too, although her cinnamon buns had elicited a good deal more enthusiasm. The memory of Colin sitting at her kitchen counter and grunting over her buns made her skin sizzle.

Quietly she slipped into the chair beside him and waited, breathing in the smell of his cologne. Funny, it was different than the scent he'd worn the other day. This one was nice, but she preferred the other. Then she forgot all about his cologne and her nervousness as she observed the expressions he made—from curious to puzzled to…pained? Wow, he took his job seriously, that was for sure. When Colin blurted something out loud, Daisy could barely contain her laughter. It took a rare individual to sit alone in a crowded restaurant with his eyes closed, muttering away to his heart's content. People had been committed for less.

"It's saffron."

Colin's eyes flew wide open, looking completely startled by her presence. "I'm sorry. What did you say?"

"You were wondering what was in the cream sauce and I said saffron." She grinned.

"How exactly did you know what I was thinking?"

Daisy leaned forward and whispered, "Because you were *thinking* out loud."

"I see."

"You know, all you have to do is read the menu and you'd know what was in there. See?" She slid a menu across the table and pointed to the description of the halibut.

Colin snatched the menu from her and closed it firmly before setting it on the corner of the table farthest from her. "Thank you, but I prefer to let the ingredients speak for themselves. Reading the menu creates bias."

Taken aback by his tone, Daisy blinked and then smiled. "You know, I do *exactly* the same thing."

"Is that right?" He gave an impatient sigh. "I'm sorry, but I really need to get back to work."

Daisy stared. What was wrong with him? Where was the banter? The sexual innuendo? He was all serious and curt and uptight tonight.

"Is there something else I can do for you?" he asked in a tone that could only be described as haughty.

"I just wanted to thank you," she said slowly.

"Thank me?"

"For the article. The review."

"The review?"

"Nana Sin's?" His blank stare made her blather on. "It was wonderful. The review—I mean, the article. I framed it and put it up in the bakery. You called it 'sinfully delicious.'" God, how she hated herself. But Colin's cold tone and demeanor had awoken the insecure child in her. She suddenly felt annoying, inadequate and unattractive.

He blinked once then twice and then slowly—as if he had to make himself do it—smiled. It bore no resemblance to the crooked, wolfish smile he'd worn indiscriminately in her kitchen just a few days ago.

"Ah, yes. Now I remember. Nana Sin's Bakery." Colin tapped his pencil against his notepad and then pointed it at her. "Rose, isn't it?"

"Daisy."

"Right. Daisy Sinclair." He nodded while smiling politely. "I'm glad you liked it."

Bile rose in Daisy's throat as she realized with horror that she'd been duped. Colin Forsythe had not only forgotten her name but also played her for a fool in the worst possible way. How could he?

"You never meant those things you said, did you?"

"What things?"

"You know, after you saw me naked." Her lip quivered and she prayed that the anger growing in her belly would sustain her long enough to keep the stupid tears at bay. "The stuff about me being delicious and curvy and perfect. It was all a load of crap, wasn't it?"

Colin stared at her with his mouth hanging slightly open. It was the same expression he'd worn when he walked in on her. Only this time his eyes didn't twinkle.

"I suppose asking me out to the gala was all a ruse, too. Well, you know what? I don't need a pity date. I..." She had to stop talking because her chin was trembling, which meant only one thing. Tears were right behind.

Damn him!

Colin dropped his pencil. "I would never ask you out on a pity date."

"No? Then what was it?"

"A mistake."

"A mistake?" Daisy had had enough. If she'd thought Colin catching her in the raw was the worst humiliation she'd suffered, she was wrong. His snub was worse. Much worse.

JAMIE FORSYTHE PORED over the documents from his latest client. The woman had no idea what she was entitled to in a divorce. She was just eager for it to be over because of her asshole husband. Reading between the lines, Jamie had to wonder why she was in such a hurry to get out. His gut told him there was more going on. Some reason for her to want to up and leave, asking for nothing, just needing out. His mind automatically went to domestic violence.

Shit. These were the worst files, and Jamie hated them. Yet these were also the cases that gave his job meaning: the quicker Jamie could help his client leave an abusive relationship, the better.

His stomach growled, alerting him to the fact that he'd worked through dinner. Again. He put the file aside, stretched his neck and rolled his shoulders. He'd grab a slice of pizza on the way to the gym. Jamie couldn't decide which need was more pressing: his hunger, which would be sated by a couple of slices of thin-crust pepperoni from his favorite pizzeria, or overcoming the restlessness he'd been feeling all week, which an hour with the speed bag before a good sparring match would hopefully alleviate. Not that it'd done the trick yet. This was going to be the fourth night in a row he'd tried.

He grabbed his leather jacket and helmet from the cupboard in his office and was on his way out the door when his cell phone rang.

"What the hell have you done?" Jamie's brother, Colin, was on the other line. Shouting.

Surprise, surprise.

The fact that Colin was five minutes older than Jamie had always made Colin feel superior.

Pinching the bridge of his nose, Jamie paused, leaning against the door frame. "I don't know, but I'm sure you're about to enlighten me."

"I just had the pleasure of meeting Daisy Sinclair."

A delicious memory of the dark-haired beauty from the bakery came to mind. "She's mine. Back off."

"Tell me, at what point in the interview did you manage to get her clothes off?"

The image of Daisy standing in her skimpy underwear, looking like some goddess from a Raphael painting about to throttle a mere mortal to death with a scale, made Jamie bark with laughter.

"One task, Jamie. One *tiny*, insignificant task. All you had to do was write a couple of paragraphs about a little out-of-the-way bakery. That was it. That's all I asked."

"You asked me—no, *begged* me—to do your job. I did it. Pretty damn well. So stop complaining."

"I didn't have a choice."

"Until you tell me why you didn't have a choice, I don't care. You asked. I helped. It's the last time. Right?"

Silence. Jamie could picture his twin brother. His head would be hanging, thumb and index finger pinching the bridge of his nose—the mirror image of himself from only seconds ago. Even in their early thirties, they were still pretty much identical. In looks, anyway, and in the fact that they both enjoyed food—but then, who didn't?

That was where the similarity ended.

"If you're accusing me of being unprofessional—"

"I'm not accusing *you* of anything," Jamie said. "You're the one who called me, accusing me of something. What it is, I have no idea."

"Do I really need to spell it out for you?"

"Please."

"You screwed my assignment."

"What are you talking about? The piece was good. Maybe a little more engaging than your stiff, pretentious drivel, but passable as your work."

"No. I mean you literally *screwed* my assignment."

"For God's sake, I didn't sleep with the woman, if that's what you're implying. Give me a little credit."

"So you didn't call her curvy and perfect?"

"Well, that part's true."

"Tell me you didn't invite her to the celebrity gala on Saturday."

"Actually, I *did* invite her."

"As me?"

"Well…" Jamie hesitated. He hadn't had the chance to explain to Daisy. Yet. He thought she'd have phoned by now—he'd given her his cell number before leaving and he'd planned on telling her the first chance they had to talk. When she didn't call, his plan had changed a bit. He was going to pick her up tomorrow, tell her who he really was, take her to the gala and point out the fact that he was the better-looking, more interesting, infinitely funnier version of Colin Forsythe. Or that Colin was the less attractive, uptight, far duller version of Jamie Forsythe. Either way, it was the first thing on his agenda, and he planned to get it out of the way so they could move on to more pleasurable activities.

"I'm hosting the gala. I can't have *you* there, masquerading as me."

"I won't be masquerading as you. You know how much I hate that whole stick-up-the-ass feeling I get pretending to be you."

"She can't know about the switch, Jamie. She could blow it for me."

"That's not my problem."

When his brother spoke next, his voice sounded tired—no, more than tired. Colin sounded exhausted and worried. "You don't understand."

"Fill me in. Then maybe I will."

"I've been offered a job as one of the hosts on *The Chicago Gourmet*. The producers are going to be at the gala."

"Congratulations," Jamie said, rubbing his jaw. "So why don't you sound excited?" The longer it took for Colin to answer, the more worried Jamie became. "What's wrong?"

His brother said something, but it was so quiet, Jamie had to ask him to repeat it.

"I said, I'm losing it."

"What do you mean, losing it?"

"My sense of taste."

"What?"

"That's where I was the other day—getting tests done."

"What about your sense of smell?"

"It seems to be going, too."

"What do they think it is?"

"They don't know yet."

Jamie let his head fall against the door frame. "Is it a tumor?"

There was a long pause before Colin repeated, "They don't know."

"Holy shit."

"No one can know, do you understand? No one."

Jamie scrubbed a hand up and down his face. "Daisy won't expose you."

"You don't know that."

It was true. Even though spending the morning with her had felt like spending time with an old friend, someone he knew but didn't know, someone he liked a whole lot and wanted to get to know even better, he really couldn't predict how she'd react to the news that he'd posed as his brother. The fact was, though he'd seen her in her tasty pink undies, he didn't know Daisy Sinclair at all.

"Look. It's not like it matters to you," Colin said.

"What's that supposed to mean?"

"You know what that means. You go through women like disposable razors. One nick and they're in the trash."

Jamie stopped pacing to stare out the window of his office. While the analogy might be fair, he still didn't like hearing it. Made him sound like an ass.

"You've got to let this go," Colin said. "Besides, it's too late."

"What do you mean, it's too late?"

"It means I already canceled the date."

"What?"

"Don't bother calling, either. She said she never wanted to speak to me—you—again. Oh, and she thinks you're a dick. Sorry."

3

DAISY CHECKED HER jacket and stood in line to get into the Grand Ballroom at the Chicago Hilton with her gala invitation scrunched in her hand, anxiety gnawing away the lining of her stomach. This was a mistake.

Why had she let Gloria talk her into this?

"You've got to go, Daisy," Gloria had said. "Go and show Colin Forsythe you don't give a damn about him, about his stupid column, about anything." Then Gloria had helped her with her hair and makeup, doing what best friends do, talking her up, telling her she looked gorgeous.

"I wish I could be there to see his face. He's going to regret his decision the second he sees you." Gloria took a couple of pictures of her followed by the obligatory selfie, and Daisy left her place feeling like a million bucks: confident, bold and daring in her new dress.

Now she felt more like a buck fifty. Conspicuously dressed in red—she apparently didn't get the memo that she was supposed to wear black—Daisy felt her face burn, no doubt matching the color of her dress, as both men and women turned to stare at her while waiting to get into the ballroom. As if to punctuate her sense of not fitting in, her mother appeared—tall, lithe and gorgeous as ever in a pencil-thin, strapless *black* dress, wearing her handsome date like an accessory on her arm. So they hadn't broken up. Daisy racked her brain for his name. What was it? Alexander? Didn't matter. Her mother's good-looking, usually much younger boy toys were all the same and never lasted.

"Seriously, Daisy?" her mother said. "Red?" She made a subtle motion with her fingertips toward Daisy's dress.

"I didn't know." One second in her mother's presence and all the insecurity came flooding back. It didn't help that her mother always looked perfect…and young…and beautiful, more like an older, more sophisticated sister than her mother. "Why didn't you tell me it was black dress only?" Daisy complained.

Tapping the invitation with her manicured nail, her mother pointed out, "It says it right here. See? Black and white."

"Oh." God, she hated this. Daisy was just about to march right back out the door when Alexander said, "I think you look nice, Daisy." The man grinned, making him look even younger than he probably was.

When her mother tried to give him her best evil eye, he laughed, and the guy looked downright boyish. "Honestly, Cyn. Don't you think everyone else here looks… kind of boring?"

"Thank you, Alexander," Daisy said cautiously.

"Call me Alex." He smiled. It even looked genuine.

Huh. Puzzling.

"Well," her mother huffed. "I'm glad you think my daughter looks nice. It would be lovely if you said *I* looked nice."

"You don't look nice. You look beautiful." He bent down and kissed her, and her mother, the ice queen, melted under his tender words. "You're so beautiful, sometimes I forget that you need me to tell you," Alex added.

Whoa. What the hell was going on? Daisy watched the interaction between her mother and Alex with equal parts interest and disbelief. It had to be an act. This was not real. Her mother was not insecure, and the guys she slept with were not considerate. Not only that—Alex had called her *Cyn*. Cynthia hated it when people shortened her name.

While Daisy was trying to figure out what game her mother and her boyfriend were playing, she found herself herded into the ballroom with all the other guests. Before she knew it, the opportunity to gracefully back out of the evening had passed.

Besides, the delicious aromas in the room had her mouth watering. She wandered the ballroom, checking out the offerings of the top thirty restaurants in Chicago, having already lost her mother and Alex, who'd stopped to chat with other members of the Arts Council of Chicago, the hosts of the fund-raiser. Though her mother had been the one who got her the invitation to the gala, Daisy was sure Cynthia didn't mind if she went her own way. The two of them had nothing in common. Never had. Never would. It was her grandmother who'd raised her, not her young, single mother, and a few minutes in each other's presence was about all either of them could handle.

Anyway, Daisy found it easier navigating the gala on her own rather than feeling like a third wheel. She surveyed the ballroom. Maybe tonight wouldn't be a complete bust; maybe it would actually be fun. And as she got caught up in the way people were milling about, talking and laughing as they mingled, eating delicious food and drinking, she *almost* forgot that she was supposed to be there with Colin Forsythe—the jerk.

Then she heard his voice.

"Good evening, ladies and gentlemen. Welcome to the

fifth annual Celebrity Hors d'oeuvres Gala. I'm Colin Forsythe, and I'll be your host this evening."

Daisy spun around, her heart in her throat. Not far from
where she stood was a stage, and behind the podium was
none other than the jerk himself, looking obnoxiously handsome in his black tux. He was standing beside a beautiful
blonde woman in a low-cut black dress that had a slit up to
her hip, showing off shapely legs and a nauseatingly perfect figure.

Daisy wanted to punch her.

Who was she? Was she his date? Was she the woman
he'd dumped her for?

As if he could read her thoughts, Colin continued, "I'd
like to introduce tonight's cohost, Tricia Gordon, producer
and host of the popular program *The Chicago Gourmet*."

"Champagne, miss?" A waiter stood at her side, holding a tray of champagne flutes.

"Yes." She swiped two glasses. The waiter moved on
and Daisy downed the first glass, the bubbles making her
sneeze so that she spilled part of the second glass on her
shoes.

She didn't care.

Tricia moved so close to Colin that they were practically
inhabiting the same space, and then she smiled up at him,
showing off perfect teeth. "It's going to be a great night.
Let me explain how this evening will go." Her voice was
clear and engaging as she spoke into the microphone. "Purchase voting chips at the cashiers located near the ballroom
exits, and then taste as many…"

Daisy tuned out what the woman was saying, hearing
Gloria's voice in her head instead.

*Go and show him you don't give a damn about him,
about his stupid column, about anything… He's going to
regret his decision the second he sees you.*

While Tricia-with-the-perfect-smile-and-body was reciting the rules for voting, Daisy was coming up with her very own plan. Colin Forsythe might not regret canceling their date, but he would regret meeting her. Daisy was going to make sure of it.

HOLY SHIT!

Daisy Sinclair was here. She was certainly easy to pick out in that incredible red dress of hers, looking like a 1950s pinup girl. Of course, that could just be his dirty mind imagining her in sultry poses, as it had all week. Didn't matter. There was no ignoring the fact the woman was a sight to behold in her red dress with the full skirt and narrow waist. The bodice was low and fitted—holy hell, was it fitted. It was a dress to go dancing in, and he could see himself leading her around the dance floor, hand on her waist, her skirt spinning so high he'd catch a glimpse of whatever pretty panties were hiding underneath.

She hadn't seen him yet, because her gaze was focused on his brother up on the stage. She watched him the way a hungry lioness watched an antelope, her cheeks flushed, her eyes blazing, her lips moving as if she was plotting his takedown. Oh, and she was drinking champagne like it was iced tea on a hot day.

What the hell had Colin said to her to get her so riled?

All Jamie wanted to do was go over there and explain the situation. At the very least, she deserved the truth. But he'd promised Colin, and now that he realized Colin's soon-to-be new boss was cohosting the evening with him, Jamie understood how delicate the situation was. It was while Tricia was extolling the importance of the Arts Council of Chicago and all the group did for the arts community that Jamie felt his phone vibrate in his tux jacket.

He pulled it out, not surprised to see a text from his brother.

She's here.

Who? Jamie texted back, in the mood to torture his brother, particularly while he was up on stage pretending to be listening to Tricia and not texting.

The Sinclair woman. Red dress. Impossible to miss.

You sure?

Yes, I'm sure.

So?

Do something.

I'll tell her the truth.

No!

Pretty hard when there are two of us here.

There's a break in five minutes. Do it then.

Are you serious?

No scenes.

Sometimes Jamie felt the very thing his brother needed was a scene. But then he remembered the pain and fear in Colin's voice when he spoke to him on the phone the other night. He thought about the possibility that his brother might have a tumor. What if it was cancer? The Cajun chicken taco he'd just eaten churned in the pit of his stomach. His brother might drive him crazy at times, but he was the only family Jamie had left, and the idea of the world without his brother in it was too much for him to contemplate. It couldn't happen. He wouldn't let it. Not after he'd lost Sarah. Jamie wasn't about to lose another sibling.

In the meantime, he would do what he had to do to make sure the lovely Daisy Sinclair didn't create a scene...or worse, commit murder.

DAISY HAD JUST consumed enough liquid courage to approach the stage, except as she neared, Colin ducked out a side door. Damn. Now she'd have to chase him. Not that he should be hard to find. The guy towered over most everyone. Once out in the lobby, however, Daisy realized she needed to make a stop at the ladies' room first, as the champagne had gone right through her.

And she needed to compose herself.

Standing in front of the restroom mirror, Daisy stared at her reflection, practicing the words she was going to say. She noticed her lipstick had worn off, so she reapplied it—though it took a couple tries before she got it straight—and she found she had to hold on to the counter as the room began to spin.

"Are you okay?" An older woman using the sink beside Daisy peered at her with concern. "You didn't eat those raw oysters, did you? They're food poisoning in a shell is what they are."

"No," Daisy said, her stomach feeling queasy at the thought.

"A cool cloth to the back of the neck should help."

Daisy hung her head for a second before splashing cold

water on her cheeks, thinking how much the woman reminded her of Nana. When she lifted her head, the woman
was gone. Strange, Daisy didn't hear her leave. That was a
bad sign because it meant she was on the *too* side of tipsy.

When she walked out into the hallway, there was Colin,
leaning against the wall, looking casual and handsome and
sexy with his longish hair tamed back for the evening. His
presence was such a shock that even though it had been
Daisy's intention to look for him, now that he was here,
apparently waiting for her, she experienced an irrational
urge to flee.

"Daisy Sinclair. What a nice surprise."

"Really?" She lifted her chin and crossed her arms over
the snug bodice of her dress. "Somehow I got the impression you didn't want me here."

"Whatever gave you that idea?"

"Hmm." She tapped her lips. "Could have been when
you said it was a mistake to ask me to come."

"Oh. That." At least he had the good grace to look sheepish. "Bad day. Let me take you home."

"I'm not going home. I haven't even eaten yet."

"We'll stop somewhere on the way."

"What are you talking about? You're the emcee. You
can't leave."

Colin made a dismissive gesture toward the ballroom.
"Tricia can handle it." His laissez-faire attitude reminded
her of the first day they'd met.

Daisy cocked her head and stared hard at the man. While
he was a little fuzzy around the edges, he wasn't that fuzzy.
"What is going on?"

"Nothing."

Taking a step closer, Daisy leaned in. She didn't know
what possessed her, but she sniffed him. She closed her
eyes and sniffed again. His cologne was the same as the

day in the bakery. Except there was a hint of Cajun spice on his breath, too. She took a step back and squinted up at him. When had Colin had a chance to eat? He'd been up on stage all evening. Daisy turned her attention to his face and hair. Something was different about his hair. The longish bits curled around his ears, soft and inviting.

"Daisy? Is something wrong?"

"You know," she said tentatively, "you've got the most interesting hair."

"What do you mean?"

"It was long at the bakery. And then short at the restaurant. And here it is, a little longer again. You must be like one of those things from the Dr. Seuss books that have to get a haircut every day."

He licked his lips, a panicky expression taking hold of his features. "You're drunk."

"No. I'm not."

"Let me take you home."

"Who are you?"

Colin pinched the bridge of his nose. "If I promise to tell you the truth, will you come with me?"

She'd barely said yes when something behind her made Colin's eyes widen. Then he grabbed her arm and pulled her toward the exit, but not before she peeked over her shoulder just in time to see a second—almost identical—Colin Forsythe watching them leave.

4

SHE SHOULD HAVE taken a cab home.

Of course Colin rode a motorbike. Of course. Because motorbikes were like cinnamon buns—Daisy's other weakness.

Wait a second!

Not Colin. *Jamie.* That was what he'd said his name was. Jamie Forsythe, Colin's twin.

It was *Jamie* who'd come to Nana Sin's, posing as his brother. Of all the immature, juvenile, childish stunts, posing as a twin took the cake. It was *Jamie* who'd shamelessly flirted with her. Jamie who'd invited her to the gala.

Outrageous!

I'm sorry, Daisy. I was going to tell you first thing.

Yeah, right.

Now here she was, stuck on the back of his KTM Super Duke—a stupidly hot bike—fuming. Sort of.

Trying to.

Except that she could hardly catch her breath. Jamie took the corners so sharply, both of them leaning together as the pavement whipped by. The wind was rushing against her cheeks and through her hair, and the powerful engine was sending confusing vibrations from the seat up into her body. It was all too much. Not to mention the way Jamie had tucked her skirt so carefully around her legs.

Why could she still feel his fingers on her thighs?

Daisy shifted on the seat, pressing herself closer to the man in front of her to the point that she could feel his hard muscles move, even beneath the leather of his jacket.

Rubbing her cheek against the supple leather, she drew in a leisurely breath.

Ah, leather. Was there anything more masculine than its scent?

This was bad. She had it bad. Daisy should probably see it as a sign that Colin—no, not Colin, Jamie, sheesh!—rode a motorbike. But a sign of what? That motorcycles revved up her girlie parts? Or that she had a penchant for making big mistakes after sitting on the back of one? Hadn't her first date with Alan started on the back of a motorcycle?

Jamie pulled the bike over to the curb and turned his head. His eyes flashed with the reflection of the streetlight before going dark. "Are you okay?"

"Yes."

"You sure?" His lips twisted in a sexy smile.

Sexy smile? Honestly, Daisy. The man's a liar. A no-good, dirty-rotten liar. He is absolutely not *sexy.*

"Of course I'm sure. Why?"

Suddenly Jamie's hands covered hers and Daisy realized something. Something critical and troubling.

Slowly, slowly she eased her hands out from under Jamie's, which meant drawing them out from beneath his jacket—worse—from beneath his shirt.

How the hell had she managed to work her hands up under his shirt?

"I think you should take me home." Daisy's fingers twitched from the loss of Jamie's warm skin—and his rock-hard abs.

The man flashed an even more sinful smile. "Let's eat first. Then I'll take you home." He motioned with his head toward the building they were stopped in front of. Some little mom-and-pop pizzeria.

Yes, food was a good idea. A very good idea.

He swung his leg over the bike and held his hand for Daisy as she stepped down onto one wobbly leg, attempting to dismount as he had. Unfortunately, her skirt got caught and the whole thing was done with no grace at all. Once on the sidewalk, she looked up to find Jamie sporting a perfectly wicked grin.

"What?" Daisy asked, trying unsuccessfully to extract her hand from his.

"Nothing."

"Tell me why you're smiling like that." She tugged again. He still didn't let go.

"You don't want to know."

"Yes, I do," she said, even though she realized—too late—that maybe she really didn't want to know. But Daisy had no time to reconsider because Jamie hauled her close and looked down at her from all that ridiculous height. "You wear the nicest panties."

With a gasp, she shoved him away. "Perv!"

"Hey, don't blame me. You're the flasher."

Daisy groaned.

Laugh lines appeared at the corners of Jamie's eyes. "That's twice, Ms. Sinclair. If I didn't know better, I'd think you were doing it on purpose."

She smacked him on the arm, and Jamie's features went through a transformation as he tilted his head to the side, blinking, studying her as though he'd just discovered her. Every muscle, every tissue and cell in her body went still, as if they were caught in stop-motion animation and it would take someone to manipulate her in order for her to move again. Someone named Jamie, ducking down to give her a kiss, for example.

A kiss? What the hell was she thinking? She did not want to kiss Jamie-the-liar Forsythe. Uh-uh.

Maybe she *was* a little tipsy.

She cleared her throat. "You know what? I *am* hungry."

With his hand on the small of her back, feeling weirdly possessive—which he had absolutely no right to be, but Daisy allowed it for some stupid reason—Jamie directed her into the tiny restaurant, where there were only seven tables covered in checked cloths and lit by candles stuck in old wine bottles.

It was wonderfully cozy and horribly romantic. Not what Daisy needed in her current state of distraction.

Jamie held her chair, and the second she sat down, a plump Italian woman bustled out through the swinging kitchen doors, her hair wrapped in a scarf, her arms outstretched to give Jamie a hug and a peck on each cheek. "Back so soon?"

"You know me. I can't stay away."

"But you brought a date for once." She flicked her hand in Daisy's direction. "If you're not careful, Jamie, you'll make Rosa jealous." The woman turned to face Daisy, eyes sparkling in a rosy-cheeked face. The woman's words were contradicted by the way she winked and then leaned close to press Daisy's cheeks between her soft hands. "So nice to meet you. Why hasn't Jamie brought you here before?"

"I—"

"Rosa, this is Daisy Sinclair."

"What a beautiful name. A flower, like me."

"Thank you. Nice to meet you," Daisy replied slowly.

As Jamie took his seat—not across from her, oh no, right beside her—he said in a stage whisper, "It's our first date."

"No," Daisy said. "This isn't a—"

"Oh!" Rosa's smile lit up her already shining eyes. "Then I know just what to make for you. House special. No problem." She scurried back to the kitchen as if on a highly important mission.

"Let's get something straight," Daisy said, inching her chair away. "This isn't a date."

"Says the girl who couldn't keep her hands off me."

Daisy raised a finger in protest, but she had no comeback. Changing the subject seemed like the only option. "You come here often, I take it."

"My office is right around the corner."

"Your office?" She moved back more. "So, tell me, now that we both know you're not a food critic, what is it that you do, *Jamie*?" Emphasizing his name seemed like a good way to remind him—and her—that she was mad at him.

"I'm a lawyer. Forsythe, Murphy and Burgess."

"A lawyer, huh? I knew I shouldn't trust you."

"Hey, I said I was sorry."

Yes, he had. Three times, but…she blinked. "What did you say the name of your firm was?"

Jamie repeated the name.

"Huh. That sounds familiar."

"Well, it is my name. And Colin's."

"True." Daisy squinted as she studied Jamie in the candlelight, trying to suss him out. "You don't look like a lawyer."

"What do I look like?"

"I don't know. A NASCAR driver?"

He chuckled. It was a nice sound—deep and rumbling.

"What's so funny?"

"You say and do the most unexpected things."

Daisy finished the glass of water, hoping to hide her smile. His observation wasn't necessarily that flattering and yet…the way he'd looked at her when he said it, well, it made her feel…hot. And the ice in her drink didn't do a damn thing about the heat creeping up the inside of her tummy, through her chest and up her throat. She had to do something about her body's involuntary reaction to Colin.

No!

Jamie.

She could not forget about that little setup. Sitting straight in her chair and holding a hand to her tummy in hopes of quelling the heat, Daisy said, "So, you pose as Colin often, do you?"

"No."

He slid his chair closer so that their thighs were touching.

She nudged her chair in the opposite direction. "But you did last week."

"Yes."

Every time she moved away he pressed closer and, wow. The guy was solid granite. She cleared her throat. "Isn't that, oh… I don't know." She tapped her lips. "Sort of juvenile?"

"Probably." He reached into her lap, picked up her hand and kissed the back of her knuckles in a move similar to the one he'd pulled in the shop. She let him.

"Do you want to tell me why you did it?" The question came out in a weird, breathy voice.

"No."

Daisy considered Jamie's one-word answers, or tried to, which was hard because he was still holding her hand, caressing her knuckles, and it seemed like the most natural thing in the world. Plus his leg was moving, up and down, up and down, and it felt so damn good.

God. It had been too long. That was her problem: she hadn't had sex in far too long, which was why she was responding to Jamie in this uncharacteristically flirty way. The question was why was Jamie being so forward? Why was he coming on to her? Was he really trying to seduce her? Or was he just feeding her more lies to cover up what he and his brother had done?

Suddenly a thought dawned. "Is it the bakery?"

He blinked. "Is what the bakery?"

"Did your brother think it was beneath him to review some stupid bakery?" That would certainly explain Colin's disdainful attitude toward her in the restaurant.

As Daisy stared into Jamie's face, she tried to conjure up the hurt and rejection she'd felt while sitting across from Colin at Le Beau Monde. The problem was the candlelight accentuated the hollows of Jamie's cheeks, drawing attention to the fullness of his sensual lips and giving his eyes such an unholy and sinful glow that she could no longer picture Colin.

Only Jamie.

Staring directly into her eyes, he said, "I swear to you this had nothing to do with you or the bakery. I only did it because my brother needed me. For personal reasons." He squeezed her hand. "That's the truth."

Or so he claimed. It was hard to believe someone who probably hadn't said one word of truth to her from the moment they'd met and who was currently distracting her with soft caresses on the inside of her wrist. Yet, when she was able to focus, there was something in his face—the seriousness of his expression and the way his eyes had lost their sparkle—that told her he wasn't lying. "And for the record, every word I wrote about your bakery was the truth. It's a gem and you should be proud."

She chewed on her lip as quotes from his review played over in her mind. *Daisy Sinclair, who is as sinfully delicious as the bakery itself...*

Yeah, okay. Maybe she'd memorized the article. So what? The bakery was a gem and she was proud.

"Look, Daisy, I'm really sorry about everything. This is not how I planned for tonight to go."

"No? So, what was your plan?" Daisy tried to maintain the snark in her voice but failed miserably.

"I was going to pick you up, tell you who I really was and then take you out on the best date of your life."

"Really?"

"Yes."

Why was her hand still in his? "Tell me about it."

"We would have left the gala early to go dancing."

"Dancing?" The squeeze she gave was involuntary, a reflex to the fact that she loved dancing. That was all.

"I know this great little salsa club." He eyed her outfit. "That dress is meant for dancing." His gaze lingered appreciatively on her neckline.

Normally Daisy would be incensed by such blatant ogling, but tonight? She didn't mind. "And then?"

"Then—" he glanced around the restaurant "—I was going to bring you here."

"So we're back on track."

"I hope so."

Daisy finally managed to extricate her hand from Jamie's and leaned back, trying to work herself up into feeling angry, the way she'd felt earlier in the evening. She tried to recreate the urge to claw his eyes out, which was how she'd felt seeing him up on stage beside Tricia Gordon. But that had been Colin, not Jamie.

She *should* want to claw Jamie's eyes out, too, for lying to her.

But she didn't. Not one bit. Instead of wanting to claw his eyes out, she had the urge to run her fingernails up his bare back.

Instead of feeling angry, she had fluttery whatnots salsa

dancing in her stomach and throbby do-das doing the merengue between her legs.

Her body was primed for dancing—dirty dancing—and while Daisy prepared a whole statement in her head, something like, *Nice try, buddy. While I appreciate your apology, it's going to take a hell of a lot more than that to get me to forgive you*, the words stayed lodged at the back of her throat.

And then something happened to distract her from attempting to say the things she should have said. The most amazing scents wafted out of the kitchen—pesto, garlic, basil, olive oil, fire-roasted tomatoes on fresh, thin crust—as Rosa opened the door, carrying a pizza round at shoulder level. Daisy's mouth watered, alerting her to the fact that she was starving. Maybe some food would help her gain a little rationality, too.

Because at the moment, with Jamie Forsythe's leg pressed so intimately against hers and his insolent gaze burning her cheeks, Daisy was about to do something completely and utterly irrational.

WHY HAD HE brought Daisy here? He never brought dates to Rosa's. This was his place.

But Jamie would do it all over again simply to watch Daisy eat. The woman certainly appreciated good pizza. Was there anything sexier than that?

Yes.

Daisy's red dress and the black panties that were hiding underneath.

But watching Daisy eat Rosa's specialty, the Margherita pizza, was pretty damn sexy. The slow deep breaths she took with each and every bite, consuming the food with all her senses. The way her eyes fluttered closed as she chewed, the little sounds of pleasure that escaped her—she probably had no idea she was making them.

The woman was having a love affair with his favorite pizza.

An image of Daisy's naked body moving—no, writhing—beneath him while she made those sounds, flashed so vividly across his brain that Jamie choked on his slice.

"You okay?" she asked, covering her full mouth.

"Fine."

Liar. He was not fine. Not one bit. This woman, whom he barely knew, had an effect on him the likes of which he'd never experienced before. The rare combination of innocence, forthrightness and sensuality she projected brought out conflicting emotions in Jamie. On the one hand, he wanted to take care of her. Protect her. Keep her away from all the dickheads in the world.

Guys like him.

On the other hand...

Dammit. He fought the urge to back her against the wall, flip up her skirt, tear off those panties and take her, right here, right now.

Hard.

Jesus. It was insane.

"Do I have sauce on my face?"

"What?" Jamie asked.

"You keep staring at me. Am I covered in sauce?" She wiped her mouth. "God, this is so good."

"No. You're fine." He hoped she didn't hear his groan. The woman was better than fine. She was—Daisy licked her lips, her tongue sweeping over the plump, pink surface of her mouth, leaving nothing but a damp sheen behind—*evil*, that was what she was. Licking her lips like that? Pure evil.

It took every ounce of control not to grab her chin, pull her face close and taste those lips for himself.

Claim them.

She leaned toward him wearing a frown. What the hell was she doing?

"Actually, you've got a little bit—" she wet her napkin with that dangerously evil tongue of hers and reached for him "—right there." She wiped his nose. "Got it."

The woman had just given him a spit bath and had somehow made it sexy. With her so close—oh God, he could smell her, delicious and sweet, so incredibly sweet—Jamie lost it. His hand went to the back of her head, threading through the dark curls that had fallen loose during the ride to the restaurant. He tilted her the way he wanted her and kissed her, surprising her so that her mouth parted in shock, giving him free access to her luscious warmth.

Daisy tasted better than he could have imagined. Sweet and salty, soft and wet. At first he thought she might push him away, so he held on more tightly because he wasn't done. Not even close.

But she didn't push him away.

Daisy went from pressing her palms flat against his chest to gripping his shoulders to finally twining her fingers around his neck, holding him just as firmly as he was holding her. If he'd been confused about the signals she had been sending, there was no confusion now. Her lips moved as enthusiastically as his. Her tongue danced willingly between their mouths, tangling indulgently with his. Beckoning him inside. A temptress he could not deny.

"All packed now and ready to go. No problem. You pay me tomorrow, okay?" Rosa's cheerful grin was hard to focus on because Jamie's eyes were still glazed over from the kiss.

Was it a kiss? Jamie wasn't sure because it felt more like their mouths had just had hot, sweaty sex.

"Wow." Daisy sat back, touching her lips, her eyes wide in disbelief.

She felt it, too? God. Jamie stood, holding out his hand for Daisy to take. "Come on. Let's go."

"Where are we going?" she asked, looking dazed.

"Home."

"Oh. Okay."

"And, Daisy?"

"Yes?"

He draped his jacket around her, loving the way it hung from her feminine shoulders.

Mine.

"Between here and there, you need to decide if you want me to come up."

"I do?"

"Yes."

The cool Chicago evening greeted them when they walked out the door. Daisy paused beside the bike, looking up at him with an intoxicating mixture of wonder and wantonness. "What will happen if you come up?"

He leaned down and kissed her softly, exhibiting way more control than he had any right to show. "Dessert."

"Oh. Well, there's lots of that. Pie, chocolate torte, lemon meringue. What would you like?"

"You."

5

WHAT WOULD YOU LIKE?

You...

The words played on a loop in Daisy's brain for the duration of the fifteen-minute ride back to her place, intermixed with moments from THE KISS. That was how Daisy thought of it: in big, bold capital letters.

She had never, *ever* been kissed like that.

Oh, she'd been kissed. But that kiss? Sweet Hannah, that kiss had been something else.

It had felt primal, the way Jamie took hold of her, moving toward her with authority, sliding his mouth and tongue across her lips...past her lips. The man had owned her mouth, and while at first she'd been shocked, she'd soon allowed it.

Encouraged it.

Craved it.

Now he was asking if she wanted more, and apparently a crowd of tiny beings had set up shop between her ears, because they were singing a chorus of "Yes! Yes! Yes!" in three-part harmony.

By the time Jamie pulled the bike up in front of Nana Sin's, the combination of the ride—fast and impatient—and the memory of the kiss—slow and sexy—had left Daisy's whole body throbbing. *Boom, boom, boom*, as though her heart was a bass speaker at a rock concert.

She was about to have sex. With Jamie Forsythe.

What?

She barely knew him. Not that she hadn't imagined it many times before the whole Colin/Jamie thing, but...

Don't overthink it, Daise. You're hot for him. He's hot for you. Now go upstairs and get some.

"Yes! Yes! Yes!" piped up the people in her brain.

"Quiet," Daisy whispered. She needed to think without the voices in her head distracting her.

"What did you say?" Jamie asked as he dismounted.

"Nothing."

Instead of giving Daisy his hand, he leaned close, wrapped his strong hands around her waist and lifted her up and over the motorbike. As if she weighed nothing at all.

It was the sweetest, sexiest, most manly thing anyone had done for her.

Ever.

You don't expect me to carry you across the threshold, do you? An uninvited memory of her ex-husband on their wedding night flashed inside Daisy's head, and insecurity swept over her. Once the image faded, she found herself staring up into Jamie's face. His eyes were dark with forbidden, seductive promises.

"You decided?"

She swallowed, or tried to, at least. "Can I think about it some more?"

He reached out to smooth her totally out of control hair. "If you have to think about it, the answer is no." He kissed her softly and straddled the bike again, starting it up and revving the engine.

No!

He released the kickstand.

"Wait."

He turned. "What?"

Daisy shrugged out of the jacket she was wearing. "Your jacket."

"Keep it."

"I can't do that."

"Just until next time."

Until next time.

Why did those words both thrill and sadden her?

Because she didn't want *next time*. She wanted right now.

"Jamie?"

"Yes?"

She bit her lip. "I'm glad you and Colin are different people."

He grinned. "You and me both."

She sidled closer. "And I…I forgive you for posing as him."

"Good," he said, and Daisy focused on his lips—such nice lips—as he spoke. "But I'm not sorry I did it. Not one bit."

She raised her gaze to his. "Me, neither," she said softly, resting her hands on his shoulders.

When he spoke next, the words seemed to come out of his mouth in slow motion. "Can I see you Monday?"

"Monday?" The word emerged, a tangible thing that Daisy could have touched if she wanted to.

"Yes." The single syllable seemed to stretch on forever.

Why was everything moving so slowly? Daisy leaned down. "Monday would be nice." She slid her hand to his chest, needing to feel the rumble of his deep voice within. Needing—

"Daisy?"

"Hmm?" She reached for his jaw, all rough against her

fingertips. Such a nice jaw. Such a nice face. And his lips? God. So, so nice. She ran her thumb along his full lower lip.

"What are you doing?"

"This." She closed the distance and kissed him softly, her lips barely touching his. Mmm. He smelled good. This was how he'd smelled that very first day. This was the man she remembered.

"Daisy…"

And then it was happening again.

THE KISS.

He threaded his fingers through her hair, gripping, holding her firmly in place, turning a soft kiss into something more. Their mouths enacted the crushing need that had been brewing between them since the moment they'd met. Jamie's mouth slanted over hers, licking, nibbling, biting, asking without words for her to tell him what she wanted. Demanding she give him the truth this time.

His tongue swept over her lips and into her mouth, taunting her with a preview of what might come if she was to invite him upstairs.

Heaven help her, she wanted what might come. Badly.

"Daisy," he moaned, the word sounding like it was the cause of acute pain.

"Don't leave," she whispered into his mouth, wanting to put him out of his misery…or share in it. "Please come up."

OH, THANK GOD.

Jamie had geared himself up to drive away—after making sure Daisy was safely inside her apartment—but that was not what he wanted. Not at all. Jamie wanted Daisy in a way that made it hard to think, hard to be reasonable. Impossible to be chivalrous. The urge was more than just an urge for sex. It was…

To be honest, Jamie had no idea what it was. All he

knew was it was powerful, and waiting for Daisy to unlock
the outside door of the building was taking too long. He
wanted to pick her up, throw her over his shoulder, kick in
the bloody door, carry her upstairs—if they even made it
that far—and slake this need that had him unable to think
about or focus on anything other than getting Daisy naked.

"Sorry, stupid key."

"Here, let me."

"No. I got it."

The door swung open, and Jamie followed Daisy into
the entrance and up the narrow staircase to the apartment
above the bakery. Thankfully it didn't take her quite as long
to unlock the second door as the first.

With his hand on her back, he followed her inside, shut
the door and spun her around.

"This is crazy," Daisy whispered, dropping the jacket
and reaching for him. She stood on her tiptoes and kissed
him.

"So crazy." He sifted his fingers through her hair—so
soft. He kissed her in a way that was not so soft but that
she seemed to like, based on the sounds she was making
and the way she pressed her body against him.

When Daisy pulled away, he steeled himself for her to
change her mind, even though the desire that infused her
face was surely a reflection of his own. He touched her
cheek. "Are you sure about this?"

She nodded while panting sweetly. "You?"

"Am I sure?" He wrapped an arm around her waist,
holding her against him. Could she feel him? She must be
able to, he was so hard. "You make me crazy. You know
that, right?"

Her clouded eyes said no.

"From the moment I saw you at the gala, in this dress."
He ran a finger along the top of the bodice, dipping inside

the low neckline—man, she had the softest skin. "All I could think about was peeling it off of you."

She sucked in a breath when he dipped lower inside her lacy black bra. "I've been dying to know." Her nipple hardened under his brief touch.

"To know what?"

He tilted her head back, exposing her throat. "What you taste like."

"You're kidding," she whispered.

"Nope." He kissed just beneath her jaw and licked her neck. God. So sweet.

"Mmm."

"Cotton candy." He inched back to look at her.

Her lids were heavy, her lips parted, her cheeks flushed. Absolutely fucking gorgeous.

"Then you flashed those sexy black undies." His hand slid down her back to cup her ass through her skirt. Wow. Nice ass.

A little *eep* slipped out of her mouth.

"And all I've been able to think about is ripping those suckers off."

"Ripping?"

"Does that offend you?"

She shook her head back and forth, three little shakes that made her sexy, messy hair bounce around her shoulders. "I like ripping," she said softly.

Oh, God.

Taking her face between his hands, he leaned down and kissed her again. Her lips were so soft. Soft, wet and inviting. Responsive, too. He was willing to bet that other parts of her would be the same. He led her into the tiny living room divided from the kitchen by a breakfast counter. After lifting her up onto the counter, Jamie snaked one hand possessively around the back of Daisy's neck and worked the other up under the skirt of her dress. Her bare legs felt like silk, especially high up on the inside of her thigh.

"Jamie."

He swallowed his name, wanting to keep everything this woman did and said for himself.

No one but me.

Such a strange thought, but it passed quickly because his only focus was what lay beyond that delicate skin of her upper thigh. His found the edge of her panties and somehow, miraculously, stopped himself from working his fingers under the elastic to discover the treasure hidden inside. When she wriggled her ass toward his hand, in invitation not only to explore but to plunder, he gripped the inside of her thigh in an attempt to maintain control.

"Ahh," she moaned, arching toward him in encouragement.

"Daisy?"

"Yes?"

"Where's your bedroom?"

Her eyes slid open. "Down the hall. Why?"

"If we don't go there right now, I'm going to take you here on this counter."

Her response was to start kissing him again, as though she wanted him to take her on the counter. But that wasn't what Jamie wanted.

Actually, he did want her on the counter. In fact, it was killing him how badly he wanted it. But it wasn't good enough for their first time. He wanted Daisy beneath him. Her naked body flush with his, her legs parted for him, her hair spread out over the pillow, her mouth and pussy... all his.

Shit!

Scooping her up off the counter, he carried her down the hall because he needed her right now.

WAS IT WICKED to wish that Jamie had taken her on the kitchen counter? It had always been a fantasy of Daisy's, and she had thought it might come true tonight. Jamie had seemed willing enough. But then he'd picked her up and carried her down the hall—also tops on Daisy's fantasy list—and she forgot all about the counter. Once inside her bedroom, he set her down on her feet, and Daisy went to the night stand to turn on her lamp. When she turned, Jamie was there, towering over her. How the hell did he do it? How did he make her feel so…feminine? With his hands on her shoulders and his smoldering gaze never wavering, he slowly turned her around, swept her hair to one side and eased the zipper of her dress down. She shivered, not from cold but from the way he trailed a finger down her spine with every inch the zipper lowered until it was all the way down and his fingers swept back up her backbone before dropping away.

"Take it off."

The words were soft. Commanding. Delicious. Her skin responded as if he'd tickled her with a feather, and she trembled as she shrugged the dress from her shoulders and wriggled it over her hips. It pooled around her feet.

"Wow."

Was that reverence in his voice? No. Couldn't be.

She had no time to think about it as he turned her to face him again, hands on her hips, fingers slipping beneath the waistband of her panties.

"I can't decide if I want you to take those off or leave them on."

Daisy couldn't decide, either. In fact, she couldn't think—she was too busy focusing on breathing, because it suddenly seemed like hard work.

"Leave them on. Lie down."

She obeyed. Why? Who knew. Maybe it was the tone of

his voice. Maybe it was the fact that her legs weren't willing to hold her up much longer.

She crawled onto the bed and lay on her back, arms
stretched above her head, one knee bent. Watching, waiting, reminding herself to breathe.

Jamie stood at the foot of the bed, looking down at her,
eyes hooded. Very, very still. Like a predator before it
pounced.

Please pounce. Please don't torture me any longer.

But he didn't move. He simply stood there, staring.

"Why are you still dressed?" she asked, pushing herself
up onto her elbows.

Her words broke his stillness. "Distracted," he said,
climbing onto the bed and gently pushing her back down
before running his hands up the length of her calves to her
knees, exerting pressure to open her wide. "The sight of
you lying there distracts me. You're so beautiful, I don't
want to ruin you."

"Maybe I want you to ruin me."

He pressed a kiss to the inside of her propped knee,
his hands running higher, fingers plucking at her panties,
taunting her. "Be careful what you wish for." He lifted his
head, and a thrill of excitement lanced through her at the
intensity of his gaze.

"Can you do something for me?"

"Yes."

"Show me what you like."

"What do you mean?"

He slid his hands even higher, along her waist, up her
sides to her shoulders and back down over her breasts.
"Where do you like to be touched?" He worked his fingers beneath the lace of the right cup of her bra, grazing a
nipple. "Show me how hard."

She arched toward his touch. Why show him when what

he was doing already felt so good? He skimmed his hands down her body again and sat back. "Touch yourself, Daisy. Let me watch."

With her back still arched off the bed, she reached around to undo the clasp of her bra, and once it was undone, she tossed it to the floor. His gaze never left her, and she felt it like a physical thing—a caress. Though he didn't say anything to her, his eyes directed her hands as she began kneading her own flesh, circling her nipples with her thumbs, pinching them, moaning at the sensation.

He groaned, a sound of pleasure that ignited her blood and woke a part of her that had apparently been in hibernation. She moved her hands beneath her heavy breasts and lifted them in offering to him.

Jamie made a deep rumbling sound at the back of his throat and dropped to her level, helping himself to her proffered breasts: tasting, licking, fondling them. Gentle at first, then rough. Biting and pinching, until Daisy was crying out in ecstasy.

It was all so good.

But she needed more. She needed to touch him. She needed to feel the connection of warm skin against skin, and Jamie had way too many clothes on. This time when she worked her hands up under his shirt, she knew exactly what she was doing. She knew exactly what she wanted: hot skin over solid muscle. Seriously, the man had the most amazing body, and she needed more of it. All of it.

Fumbling with the buttons on his dress shirt—stupid, tiny buttons—Daisy gave up. "Take it off, please."

He didn't listen. He just kept kissing her, devouring her as if she was his favorite dessert.

"Jamie." She tugged the material, wishing she had the nerve to rip it.

He lifted his head to look at her, his hair falling haphazardly across his forehead. He ran a thumb over her swollen lips and said, "You know what's going to happen the second I have my clothes off?"

Daisy nodded. She knew and she wanted it.

"Are you sure you're ready for that?"

Taking Jamie's hand, she pushed it down between them, between her legs, moving her panties to one side so that Jamie could touch her, sink his fingers inside her.

"Oh, baby." There was that note of reverence again. "You're so wet." He plunged inside, and Daisy held on to his hand because she could barely stand the intensity of the pleasure.

"Ah!"

With a groan, Jamie withdrew and sat back on his heels so he could finish undoing the buttons on his shirt. "Keep touching yourself, Daisy. It's the sexiest thing I've ever seen."

Happily, Daisy rubbed herself over her panties, moaning as she massaged her tight clit. Jamie's nostrils flared as he watched, his gaze leaving her body only for the time it took him to remove his cuff links. He tossed them on the nightstand before pulling his shirt off, revealing an expanse of sculpted muscle with ink covering his left pectoral muscle—not what she'd expected—and she reached for him because she had to touch. He captured her roaming hands, kissed them and placed them on his fly. Her pinkies grazed the swollen flesh hidden behind the fabric, and Daisy's body shuddered in anticipation. But before she undid his belt, she looked up. "Tell me you have condoms."

Reaching into his back pocket, he pulled out a thin wallet and removed a plastic square from inside.

"A regular Boy Scout."

His chuckle turned into a groan as she undid his belt and then his fly, reaching in to touch him for the first time.

Mercy. The man was certainly well proportioned. And hard. So, so hard. She ran her hands up and down his length, squeezing, rubbing her thumb over his tip, where a drop of moisture leaked. The rumbling sound he made encouraged her to reach deeper inside his shorts until he tugged her hand out, got off the bed and stood to remove his dress pants.

"Panties off," he ordered.

She obliged him willingly, raising her hips to push them off as he finished undressing. Standing beside the bed, he looked like a giant, a Roman god of massive proportions, perfectly sculpted, virile and all-powerful as he tore open the package and rolled the condom over his length. When he crawled back on the bed, he grabbed her wrists and held them above her head with one hand while guiding himself to her entrance with the other.

"You drive me crazy. Do you know that?" he growled.

"You may have mentioned it," she said softly, adjusting her body beneath his, parting her thighs to make room for him. This was all so surreal. Jamie drove *her* crazy—crazy with lust and impatience and desire. But for her to have the same effect on him?

That was even crazier.

6

DAISY SINCLAIR DID not drive men to distraction—

"Oh!" she cried.

With one sure thrust, Jamie buried himself inside her and all thoughts were gone. There was nothing left except sensation. The feel of him deep, the friction of movement against her channel, his bare skin against hers, chest to chest, the intensity of his gaze, which he refused to break.

A flash of something that resembled pain crossed his face as he withdrew, and for a second Daisy thought he might pull out and stop. Desperation took over, and she tried to pull him closer. "Jamie, don't."

"Don't what?"

"Don't stop."

"Oh, baby. I couldn't stop if I tried." Then he kissed her, his mouth and tongue mimicking the movement of other parts of his body, penetrating her, exploring her, delving deep inside her and filling her up to the brink, again and again and again.

Oh, this was what had been missing in her life. This was what she needed. A big, strong man to make her feel like a woman in every possible way. His body was a perfect fit, moving in and out of her with such pleasurable ease, as if she was made for him. How rare to find someone with whom she shared instant chemistry, and now to find their bodies were a match. It was unheard of. Too good to be true.

"Daisy."

Even her name was an invocation, and Daisy was completely under Jamie's spell. She held on to his powerful shoulders as his body rocked in and out of hers. She kissed his lips, his jaw, his neck, biting when he penetrated her with particular ferocity, sucking when he withdrew. The shift of his hands to her shoulders heralded an increase in tempo and Daisy met him thrust for thrust, her body awake, alive and on fire.

"Jamie!" she cried. "Oh, Jamie!"

"Come for me, baby. I need to see your face when you come."

With a cry, she dug her nails into his shoulders as her entire body contracted in shuddering release.

"Yes, Daisy. That's it. That's it." He stroked in and out once more before a final, fearsome thrust brought their quaking bodies together as deeply entwined as possible. Shuddering and pulsing, no differentiation between where one body started and the other stopped.

Gradually, the shuddering subsided. "That was amazing," she said, sighing with pleasure, her legs still wrapped high around his waist. "I could do that again."

He groaned softly in her ear. "Give me ten minutes and your wish just might come true."

THE SUN PEEKED between her shutters as Daisy lay propped on an elbow, tracing the ridges and valleys created by the muscles on Jamie's chest. She leaned closer, inspecting the tattoo that covered his heart. It was a Celtic design, a cross of some kind, and if Daisy wasn't mistaken, there was a name written in swirly script inside. She traced the script with her finger in an attempt to make it out when a contented, sleepy sound preceded movement beneath her.

Jamie's eyes fluttered open. "Good God, woman. What time is it?"

"Five-thirty."

He captured her hand, raised it to his lips and kissed it. "Go back to sleep."

"I can't."

"Why not?"

"The sight of you distracts me," she said, repeating what he'd said yesterday. "Plus you're so hard." She poked at his chest muscle, amazed at the lack of give behind his warm skin.

"Mmm." He took her hand and guided it down his body, pressing against the growing erection situated at the warm juncture between his legs. "I am."

She rewarded him with a playful slap. "Seriously. It's like you're not real. How does a lawyer get so strong?" She traced her fingers across his chest again, carefully circling another dark patch she'd mistaken for a second tattoo last night. There was another one on his shoulder. "And why are you bruised?"

He answered her with another sleepy groan.

She sucked in a breath in mock surprise. "Are you a spy?"

"Yes."

"I knew it."

Jamie moved so quickly, Daisy didn't see it coming. In one swift motion, he was on top of her, using his knees to spread her thighs, capturing her hands and pressing them into the mattress at the sides of her head. He adopted a pretend scowl. "Now give me the recipe to Nana Sin's cinnamon buns, or else."

She wriggled playfully beneath him. "Or else, what?"

He nuzzled a spot just below her chin and then lifted his head. "I'll torture you."

"Torture away," she said on a sigh. "Because I'll never tell."

He moved lower, taking a nipple into his warm mouth, and the groan that came out of him made it sound as if he was the one being tortured, not her. Wow! She loved it. Loved the feeling of the hard male flesh pressed against her thigh, loved the near desperate suction on her breast, loved the weight of him on top of her.

Loved it all.

He pulled away to say, "Lucky for you I've got one emergency condom left."

"An emergency condom?" She arched her chest toward his mouth, giving him the universal sign for *Please don't stop that thing you were just doing*. "How is an emergency condom any different from a regular condom?"

Flicking her nipple with his tongue, he said, "I could tell you, but then I'd have to really torture you."

"You don't scare me, secret agent man."

"No?" He released a hand to caress her body, licking his thumb before using it on her nipple, making slow circles. Then he took her in his mouth again.

Daisy was so absorbed in the sensations Jamie was creating that when the timer in the kitchen went off, it didn't even register until Jamie lifted his head. "What's that?"

"Oh," Daisy said, blinking and wriggling out from beneath him, pulling the sheet around her as she stood. "That's breakfast."

CHOCOLATE CROISSANTS, COFFEE, orange juice and fruit salad. It was barely six-thirty on a Sunday morning and the woman had whipped up a feast for him. The croissants were still warm from the oven: homemade pastry with rich, dark chocolate hidden inside. Decadent and delicious.

As he chewed, he gazed at Daisy sitting across the table from him. *Decadent and delicious* described her, as well. Though, as he watched her drink her coffee, he noticed she seemed to be having a hard time looking at him this morning. The uncertain woman, the one who activated the protective gene in him, was back. It was strange to see her this way, such a shift from the wildcat he'd barely been able to control between the sheets.

"You never answered my question," she said, glancing up before focusing on her coffee again.

"What question?"

"Where'd you get the bruises?"

He swallowed the pastry and chased it with a gulp of coffee. "I own a place. To work out."

"Like a gym?"

"More like a club."

"What, like a fight club?

"Kind of."

"Is it legal?"

"Is an illegal club sexy?"

"No." There was a smile hiding at the corners of her mouth.

"Liar."

Her smile broke, and it was the most beautiful thing in the world. *She* was the most beautiful thing in the world.

He rubbed his eyes. Jesus. Who was this woman? "You're bad for me, you know that?"

"Bad enough to spank?"

He dropped the croissant and stared. "Stop it."

"What?"

"You're like…the perfect woman right now."

She reached across the small table and punched him on the shoulder. Kind of hard. "Is that better?"

"Worse."

"Why?"

"Because I liked it." He grabbed her fist and held it. "And perfect women don't exist."

"Of course not, idiot. Neither do perfect men." She took a bite of croissant. "But perfection? It's real. It's fleeting, but every once in a while you can find it."

Her statement was so naively sweet, he almost wanted to believe it. They stared into each other's eyes until Jamie watched the smile fall away from her lips while her eyes clouded with something. Not the uncertainty of before, but something else.

What that something else was, Jamie didn't want to know. After slowly placing her hand back on the table, he cleared his throat, feeling desperate to escape all of a sudden. He finished his croissant in one bite and swallowed the rest of his coffee. Pushing away from the table, he glanced around, looking for something. The exit? His sanity?

His jacket was lying on the floor by the door, and he strode over to pick it up. After shrugging into it, he turned, intending to thank Daisy for breakfast. "I'd like to see you tomorrow."

What?

He hadn't planned on saying those words; they'd just come out of him. The weird thing was he didn't regret them.

"Okay," she answered softly before frowning. "I'd like that."

"Good." He exhaled the breath he hadn't realized he'd been holding. Seriously. He had to get the hell out of there before he said something else he might or might not regret. "I'll pick you up at seven."

MONDAY MORNING, JAMIE sat at his desk, staring at the pile of Dissolution of Marriage documents that needing to be filed in court for his clients. He sifted through them, figuring there were about twenty. Twenty more reminders that the idea of a permanent union between two people was a myth. Was he jaded when it came to marriage? Absolutely, and he'd lived his life accordingly.

So why did he keep seeing Daisy's face leaning over him, the sun shining around her mass of curls, sexy as sin, her smile naughty as she caressed him into wakefulness, her skin smelling warm and sweet and tasty? Why did he have the urge to repeat that wake-up call? Every. Single. Day?

The ring of the telephone was a welcome distraction, because Jamie had no answer except the unsettled feeling in his stomach. Not good.

"Hey, Jamie, it's Carson."

Jamie glanced at his watch. It was nine fifteen and Carson Murphy, his partner, should have arrived at the office forty-five minutes ago. "What's up? You sick?"

Carson coughed. Not a sick cough, an uncomfortable cough. "I'm in Florida."

"What?"

"Yeah, I know. Long story. Listen, I need you to talk to Helen about taking over my files until I sort things out."

"What's going on?" Jamie tapped his pen against the edge of the desk, thinking about how Carson had been acting strange lately. "Are you in trouble?"

"Nope. In fact, I've finally seen the light."

Jamie rubbed his temple. "Oh, God. Tell me you haven't joined a cult."

Carson laughed. "Not a cult."

"What, then?"

"I'm getting hitched."

Jamie stared at his desktop. Frozen. Finally, he said, "No, you're not."

"Yes. I am. Next week."

"This is a joke."

"No joke, man. This is the real thing."

Jamie leaned his elbows on the desk, pinching the bridge of his nose. "Jesus."

"I'm sorry to dump this on you."

Once he opened his eyes, his gaze fell back to the pile of documents on his desk. All proof that his friend and partner was making a monumental mistake. Jamie felt compelled to say it. "You're making a mistake."

"Maybe," his friend said, "but I don't care because I've never been this happy. Not even close."

After hanging up with Carson, Jamie sat back in his chair. Carson was getting married? It was impossible. Okay, obviously not impossible, but improbable, because his friend and partner was even more jaded than he was when it came to marriage.

His intercom buzzed. Helen was on the line.

"Jamie, Carson's nine-thirty appointment is here. I don't know where Carson is or what I'm supposed to tell the client."

"Carson's not coming in," Jamie said, relaying the phone call he'd just had from his partner. "Get the file together." He checked his schedule, relieved to see he was open all morning. "I'll deal with it."

Just as he hung up, a reminder bell went off on his phone. "Make reservations for dinner tonight."

Something tightened low in his abdomen as another image of Daisy—naked with messy just-had-sex hair—took over his brain. Good lord, he was going to have to be careful around her. He hadn't been this preoccupied by a woman in... God, how long? Ever?

Forgetting about Carson's client for the moment, he typed a search in Google—"most romantic restaurants in Chicago"—and scrolled through the list before finally choosing one that looked nice, but not too nice. Intimate, but not too conspicuously romantic. More importantly, it had good ratings for food.

Perfect.

No. Not perfect.

Perfection didn't exist. But that didn't mean he couldn't enjoy his time with Daisy. For now.

7

DAISY WAS LATE for her meeting. Again. As she hurried into the office building, she could hear Nana's voice in her head.

Avoiding the things you don't like doesn't make them go away. It makes them worse.

"Quiet," Daisy whispered to herself, as she exited the elevator and hurried down the hall to the "neutral" meeting room. Nana was right most of the time, but this time she was wrong. Daisy had simply forgotten about the meeting because she'd spent the morning replaying the weekend, or rather, snippets from the weekend, in her mind. Jamie's hands on her body. His mouth and tongue, too. That very, very male part of him inside her...

Lordy.

She fanned herself.

Then there was his chest. She loved his chest: the muscles, the ink, the bruises.

God. He was perfection. He might not believe in it, but he was the closest thing she'd ever found to perfection in a man. Smart, funny, tough, incredibly sexy, great in bed. And he loved her baking. Too good to be true.

If it's too good to be true, it probably is...except for when it isn't.

Daisy smiled, thinking of all the times Nana had said that over the years, always followed by her deep, throaty laugh. Well, Jamie wasn't exactly perfect. He did bolt on Sunday morning. That part was less than perfect. If it wasn't for the fact that he'd asked her out again, his hasty departure would have ruined everything.

So it was Jamie's fault she'd forgotten about the meeting today, not hers. She wasn't avoiding the unpleasantness of her divorce; she was trying to focus on pleasant things instead. Wasn't that the foundation of happiness?

Of course, *unpleasant* didn't begin to describe the dealings with her ex. Hellish torture where her fingernails were pulled out with pliers was a much more apt description.

Pausing outside the door, she could see Alan through the narrow window, looking cool, coiffed and impatient.

She curled her fist and pounded hard on the door. She did it only to watch Alan jump—which he did. With a smile, she opened the door and walked in.

Alan rolled his eyes upon seeing her. "Late and without counsel. Again. Daisy, you can't keep doing this."

She plopped herself down in the chair across from him with her old-school file folder spilling documents across the table. "We both know why I keep doing this, Alan." She placed her hands on the table and leaned forward. "There's no money left for lawyers." She looked around. "Speaking of which, where's that money-grabbing ass of yours?"

Using his chin, Alan indicated the man was standing behind her. Daisy turned.

Jamie stood in the open doorway, blinking at her in confusion. "Mrs. Smith?" He opened the file in his hands and quickly glanced through.

Daisy stood. However, her lower jaw felt like it stayed glued to the tabletop. "What the hell are you doing here?"

She glanced back at Alan, suspicion flooding her veins. "What the hell is he doing here, Alan?"

"My lawyer is out of town," Alan explained. "This is his partner." He pointed between them, frowning. "Do you two know each other?"

"No," Jamie replied so quickly that the *yes* on the tip of Daisy's tongue was swallowed before it could be uttered.

"No?"

How could such a small word—only two letters—suck the air right out of Daisy's lungs and sap the strength from her legs? She collapsed into the chair, numb, unable to do anything but stare at the man who strolled around to the other side of the table, casually sitting beside her ex-husband.

Jamie's unexpected presence had stolen her ability to breathe. His denial about knowing her had stolen her thoughts, her ability to see straight, and most importantly, her ability to hold her tears in check.

"Ms. Smith," Jamie said, looking at her from across the table. "Where is your lawyer?"

"It's Sinclair." Daisy said, her glare shooting daggers at Jamie. "And I don't have a lawyer."

Alan threw his head back and groaned. "Oh, my God! We made the agreement last month that she'd show up with a lawyer and we'd hammer out the sale of the bakery. Then we'd be done with all this." Alan leaned across the table, his face flushed with anger. "Daisy, we're not going to have anything left if you keep stalling."

She heard the words but it was impossible to process them. The only thing she was capable of was shaking her head and watching the tears drip down off her chin, blurring the court order to sell the bakery that she'd been served with two weeks ago.

Alan stood. "I was willing to bargain with you today.

But no more. One month, Daise. You give me my share of the bakery by the end of the month, otherwise it'll go to court and you won't get a dime. Do you understand?" Alan stormed around the table, muttering, "Such a waste of time. Such a waste of money," before slamming the door behind him.

JAMIE DIDN'T MOVE as he sat across from Daisy, watching her cry. At one point he shut his eyes because her tears were too painful to witness, yet listening was worse because the sounds she made reminded him of sounds she'd made a mere thirty-six hours ago, only now she was moaning out of pure misery.

"You're a bastard, you know that?" Her voice, though soft, was thick with emotion.

When he opened his eyes, he was greeted by Daisy's tear-stained face. Her nostrils flared as she struggled to take deep breaths. "How could you?" She stood, her hands shaking as she fumbled to pick up the documents strewn across the table.

Jamie hurried around the table to help. "Daisy, listen—"

She slapped his hands away. "I don't know what's worse." Her breathing was so ragged she could barely speak and her words came out in stuttering hiccups. "The fact you denied knowing me or that you're helping my ex ruin me." She made a sound, something like a half sob, half laugh, and then pressed a hand to her mouth as if that'd keep the sounds inside.

"Daisy, sit down. Please."

"Sit down with you? No, thank you." She tucked the file under her arm and turned to go.

Jamie was not about to let her leave, not in this state, and not until she heard him out. He stepped in front of her, blocking the door. "This is serious. You need to sit down, calm down and listen to me."

"Don't you dare tell me what I need." She shoved him with her shoulder as if she was a linebacker. The action surprised him enough that he stumbled out of the way, giving Daisy a chance to open the door.

He followed her out into the hall, talking quietly as they made their way to the elevator. "I've barely looked at the file, but I saw enough to know the magnitude of your situation."

She pressed the button for the elevator and stood there, completely ignoring him, blotting her cheeks with the back of her hand.

"You need to find yourself a lawyer, it's required by law, and you need to act soon. Otherwise it's going to get ugly."

Nothing.

"I know people you could call." He found his card holder and located the card of a colleague. When he held it out to her and she still didn't acknowledge him, he said, "I'm not trying to ruin you. I'm trying to help you."

The elevator doors opened and Daisy stepped inside. She turned, and when Jamie started to get on the elevator with her, she blocked his path. "If you take one step inside this elevator, I will press the emergency button and tell people you're harassing me." The last few words sounded like a hiss—harsh and final.

Jamie stood silently as the elevator doors closed. The last thing he saw was Daisy's mouth move—the very mouth he'd kissed so passionately a day ago—forming the words *I hate you* before she disappeared from view.

DAISY STOOD ON the sidewalk outside the brownstone in Old Town, looking up at the building, hating herself. Oh, there were so many reasons to hate herself right now, not the least of which was her obviously abysmal taste in men. To think she'd actually thought Jamie was different.

Perfect.

Ha!

From one asshole to another, she was destined to make poor choices as far as men were concerned.

"No more motorbikes," she muttered to herself as she made her way up the steps to the front door. "No more tattoos. No more crazy sex." Now here she was, about to grovel to the last person in the world she ever wished to grovel to. It just went to show how desperate she was.

With a sniff, she raised her chin and rang the bell.

When no one answered, Daisy experienced a brief moment of relief, until she heard footsteps and the door opened.

"Hey, Daisy," Alexander said, looking handsome in khakis and a button-down shirt.

"Sorry to just show up like this, but…"

"That's okay," he interrupted. "You looking for your mom?"

After clearing her throat, she said, "Yeah. Is she home?"

"Yep. Come on in."

Daisy followed her mother's boyfriend through the foyer, past the front sitting room and kitchen to the addition at the back of the building. She'd been here only once before, but the sun room had been her immediate favorite.

"Can I get you something? Coffee? Tea? Wine?"

"No, thank you." This was not a visit. This was a mission.

Alex motioned to the kitchen. "If you decide you want anything, make yourself at home." He left her at the door and Daisy watched him walk away. She was puzzled. He really was a nice man, and she still couldn't quite figure out what he was doing with her mother, who was typically more interested in rich men than nice men. No matter. It wasn't her business. She took a deep breath and entered the room.

Then she stopped.

Cynthia was seated by the window, wearing yoga attire and little to no makeup. Her hair was pulled back in a ponytail. But most surprising of all was the fact that she was sitting with a laptop in her lap, typing. If it wasn't for the reading glasses perched on the end of her nose, she would have looked about twenty-five. There were so many things wrong with this picture. Yoga pants? Unstyled hair? No makeup? Glasses? Working?

"What are you doing?"

Her mother's head popped up in surprise. "Daisy. I didn't know you were here." She closed the laptop and set it on the side table, then removed the glasses in a hurried motion. "What are you doing here?"

"I wanted to talk to you."

"Come in, come in." She waved her over.

Daisy approached slowly, taking the chair opposite her mother. She pointed at the laptop. "What are you working on?"

"Oh, that." Her mother glanced at the computer as if she was shocked to see it there. "It's nothing." She cleared her throat. "Well, it's silly, really. I'm writing a book, if you can believe it."

"A book?" Her mother was right. Daisy couldn't believe it. "I didn't even know you read."

Tilting her head in a show of annoyance, a pose Daisy was very familiar with, her mother said, "Of course I read. I'm not stupid."

"That's not what I meant," Daisy said, trying to find common ground with a woman she'd never been able to find common ground with before. In an attempt to make it up to her, Daisy said, "You look nice, by the way."

Cynthia made a face. "No, I don't. I just finished a workout, for God's sake." She sighed, crossing her arms over
her chest. "What do you want?"

Wow. Okay. Her mother might look different and be acting a little strange, but their relationship had obviously not
changed, and the tension between them was as potent as
ever. There was no point making nice. Daisy figured she
might as well get straight to the point. "I just came from a
meeting with Alan."

"I thought so."

"How did you know?"

"Your face." She made a circular motion in Daisy's direction. "It's all red and blotchy. You've been crying."

Daisy put her hands to her cheeks. Once again, her
mother had managed to make her feel ugly and insecure—
just like that. This was pointless. "I don't know why I
bother." She pushed herself to her feet.

Her mother's deep inhalation was audible. "Sit down.
Tell me what's going on."

Although it went against her better judgment, Daisy sat
back down, because she really had no idea where else to
turn. She slowly began to relay the sorry state of her divorce, finishing with, "I'm going to lose the bakery and I
don't know what to do."

After listening without interrupting, Cynthia said, "You
should let Alexander take a look. He's really good at this
kind of thing—he should be able to advise you."

For the first time all day, Daisy felt a modicum of relief. Could it be that she'd made the right decision to come
here and ask her mother for help? She hurried back out to
the car to retrieve her file folder. By the time she got back
inside, Cynthia had briefed Alex about what was going on.
He took the file and sat down at the kitchen table, going
through each document in great detail. In the meantime,

her mother removed a million kinds of fruits and vegetables from the refrigerator and proceeded to throw them all into a blender, creating a disgusting-looking pea-green concoction. She poured two large glasses and passed one to Daisy.

It tasted marginally better than it looked. Marginally.

"I know," Cynthia said. "It's not Nana's strudel, but it's good for you."

Daisy made a face and took another tiny sip. "So, what's the book about, anyway?"

Cynthia took a long drink, almost emptying her glass. "It's a guidebook."

"What kind of guidebook?"

"A guide to bad relationships and how to avoid them."

"What?"

Tilting her head, Cynthia said, "If you consider the men I've dated, from your father until…now, I am sort of an expert in the field of disastrous relationships." She glanced over to Alex poring over the documents, a soft smile lighting her features. "Anyway," she said, "I pitched the idea to a publisher friend of Alexander's and he liked it enough to offer me a deal. They even gave me an advance."

"Wow," Daisy said before hazarding still another sip. "That's great. Really great."

She asked her mother a few more questions about the project, and something strange happened. Her mother came alive in a way Daisy had never seen before, talking animatedly, using her hands, pacing, laughing. Making fun of herself.

Who was this woman? She was the polar opposite of the self-important, reserved person Daisy had grown up with.

"Daisy?" Alex said, gathering the papers together and placing them carefully back into the folder. "Have a seat."

Shit. She did not like the sound of his voice. Her stomach heaved, threatening to expel the horrid green drink as she slowly made her way to the table.

Once seated, Alex reached over and took her hand. "You should have come to us sooner."

Shit, shit, shit.

Swallowing was suddenly impossible.

"You don't have a lot of choices. Your grandmother left the bakery to you, but the law is clear. Property gained while married becomes part of the estate, and Alan is entitled to half of the estate." He tapped the file. "In fact, because he worked there for a number of years, you owe him a portion of the profit. You should have been paying him, but you haven't. Why?"

"There's no money. It's all gone to lawyers, bills and repairs. I had to redo the plumbing. We've been having problems with the electrical. I had to buy new stoves because there was a power surge a while back. At the end of the month, after I pay bills, there's nothing left."

Alex nodded. "These are important factors, but it's not documented anywhere. That's what you need a lawyer for." He pulled out the court order. "But the fact is it's too late. The building and bakery have been valued. It's worth three million—he's only asking for half of the worth of the building."

"Only?" Daisy interrupted, the word barely making it out of her constricted throat.

"Seven hundred fifty thousand. You need to come up with that amount in twenty-eight days."

"And if I can't?"

"The court will seize the assets and sell it." He shrugged. "It'll be a short sale and will probably go for a fraction of what it's worth."

With elbows on the table, Daisy covered her face. This

could not be happening. "I can't sell." She couldn't look up. "Nana left it to me."

"I know," Alex said softly. He paused before continuing, "God, I wish I could help, Daisy, but I don't have that much liquid at the moment."

It had always been a long shot. She glanced up.

"In six months, maybe, we might be able to do something, but—" he tapped the document again. "You don't have that much time."

A tornado whipped up inside Daisy's head, causing her pulse to crash between her ears. "I don't know what to do," she whispered. "It would kill Nana if I sold the bakery."

"Nana's already gone," her mother said quietly. "Maybe it's time you let her go."

Daisy looked up, the hopelessness of the situation mixed with the green goop her mother had fed her, making her stomach swirl. Combine that with the storm in her head punctuated by years of being ignored by her mother, years of feeling like a nuisance, and it all became too much to bear.

"You're jealous," Daisy said through clenched teeth. "You've always been jealous of my relationship with Nana."

"No."

"And you're angry that she left the bakery to me, not you."

"That's not true. I never wanted it."

"But you wanted the money." Daisy stood, a hand squeezing her windpipe, making her see spots. "That's all that's ever been important to you." She shook her head. "And here I thought you might actually be changing."

"Daisy," her mother said, standing.

"But you haven't changed. You're just as self-centered as always." Daisy pointed a finger at her mother's face. "You don't care that my life is falling apart and that the thing I love most is about to be taken away from me." She wiped the tears from her cheeks. "Do you want me to be as miserable as you? Is that what this is about?"

Cynthia didn't answer. Her face crumpled as she tried to speak. When no words came out, she shook her head and hurried from the room.

The sight of her mom scurrying down the hall didn't make Daisy feel better. It made her feel worse. A part of her—a big part—wanted to run right after her. But how many times had she done that as a child—pined after her mother, begging for attention? How many times had her mother walked away from her, in anger, annoyance or disinterest?

Too many times for Daisy to count.

"Your mother loves you, you know."

Daisy turned to Alex. "That's where you're wrong." She swept the documents from the table, wiped off the teardrops staining the top pages and placed the papers haphazardly in the folder. "She doesn't love me. She never has."

8

JAMIE SAT AT a small round table in the corner of the bakery, drinking coffee and eating a cinnamon-almond Danish that was rivaled only by Nana Sin's cinnamon buns and Daisy's chocolate croissants as the most delicious baked good he'd ever tasted. Using the free Wi-Fi in Nana Sin's, he had his laptop open and was working—the third day in a row he'd spent his afternoon there. Daisy hadn't given him any choice. She wouldn't return his calls and wasn't responding to texts or emails.

After Monday's meeting—God, what a shit show—Jamie had spent the evening going through the file. Was it a conflict of interest? Absolutely-fucking-yes. But Jamie didn't care. He wasn't about to pass this off, not even to his other partner, Lyle Burgess, because any other lawyer would screw Daisy over. It would be so easy, particularly because Daisy was being unreasonable. Despite the fact that Jamie wanted to punch Alan in the face—only because the man had had the privilege of going to bed with Daisy and waking up to her every day for four years—he had to admit that Alan had been patient while waiting for Daisy to settle.

That's why he was there. He had to talk to her. Had

to make her understand and see reason. Because if she didn't…

Breathing in the wonderful scent of fresh bread, Jamie glanced around the bakery, at the small counter, the crowded shelves of goods that would be empty by closing time, the line of people that snaked out the door. Such a successful business, one Daisy was about to lose, and that would be a tragedy. It was the only reason he was there.

Obviously their wonderful—albeit, short-lived—affair had to end. That went without saying. Which was probably a good thing. Daisy was an amazing woman, but she was the kind of woman who wanted more than what a guy like him had to offer. So it was all for the best. It really was. For Daisy, for the law firm, and for him.

Yep, all for the best.

He took a bite of the Danish he'd just ordered, and though it was delicious, Jamie had difficulty swallowing it. Taking a swig of coffee to wash it down, he noticed a bedraggled man who had just come in the door and was standing in the corner of the bakery, face lifted, eyes closed, breathing the air. Moments later, Daisy's assistant came out and passed the man a Nana Sin's bag. "Here you go, Johnny," she said.

He took the bag with a huge smile but craned his head toward the front of the shop. "Where's Daisy?"

"She's busy in the back." The woman glanced Jamie's way before returning her attention to the man. "She said to say hi and she'll see you next week."

"Tell her how much I appreciate it. As always."

"I will."

Jamie dropped his gaze, pretending as though he hadn't overheard the whole thing. So that was Johnny, the man Daisy made special buns for. Interesting.

"This isn't a library. You can't just hang out here all

day." Daisy's assistant stood beside the table, hands on her hips, her lips pressed together. "Lots of people want to sit down—you can't just take up a table for as long as you want."

"What are you going to do about it?"

The woman chewed her lip.

"I've got a suggestion. Send Daisy out to talk to me and then I'll leave."

"She won't come. I've already asked."

"Fine." Jamie stood. "Then I'll go back and talk to her."

She stepped in front of him. "I can't let you do that."

"Why not?"

A peculiar look came over her face. She glanced over her shoulder at the door leading to the back rooms. "There are a lot of knives. She's militant about keeping them sharp."

"Is that a threat?"

"Not from me." She shook her head. "But Daisy? She's… unpredictable at the moment. And, to be honest, if there's blood around the food, it'll be a health and safety nightmare."

Jamie sat back down. "Fine. I'll wait here, then."

"But—"

"Oh, and I'll have another Danish, please."

DAISY REACHED INTO the bowl, tore off another bit of dough and rolled it into a ball between her hands. There was a knock on her door but she didn't bother answering. She'd closed the door to her office to keep people out so she could think. The dough in her lap was not for baking, it was to give her something to do to help her think. Besides, it was only Lizzie, and knowing Lizzie, she'd come in whether Daisy gave her permission to or not. So why bother? Why bother with anything anymore?

The door opened, followed by Lizzie saying, "He's still here and he says he's not leaving until you talk to him."

Daisy didn't answer. She just kept rolling the soft dough until it was perfect.

"Did you hear me?"

"Yep."

She didn't bother turning her head when she heard Lizzie's footsteps approaching.

"Boss? Whatcha doing?"

"What does it look like I'm doing?"

Lizzie was now in her line of sight, wearing a perplexed expression as she blinked down at where Daisy was lying on her desk. Lizzie slowly raised her gaze to the ceiling. "Well, it kind of looks like you're losing your shit."

"Very astute."

She made a strange sound in her throat. "Um, where's your phone?"

"I don't know."

Daisy kept rolling the dough, keeping it nice and warm, nice and soft, absently watching Lizzie out of the corner of her eye. Why was she still there? "You can go now."

"In a sec." Lizzie pulled her phone from her pocket and tapped in a number. From somewhere beneath her, Daisy's ringtone went off.

"Scooch over."

Daisy shifted and Lizzie pulled the phone from beneath her. Weird, she hadn't even felt it, lodged there under her butt.

"What's your passcode?"

"I'm not telling you."

"Never mind. Got it."

Daisy grunted because, frankly, she didn't care, not even when Lizzie made a phone call using her phone.

"Gloria? No, it's not Daisy, it's Lizzie. Yeah, I'm good, but the boss? Well, she's not so good…"

Daisy located the spot she wanted and aimed.

"For starters, she's lying on her desk and throwing dough at the ceiling, if that gives you any indication."

She let fly. The dough made the most wonderful *splog* sound, and Daisy found that the more perfect the ball, the more perfect the circle of dough it created on the ceiling. The first few were irregular-shaped; the last six were lovely and round. A doughy, polka-dotted ceiling.

"Yep. Just a second." Her phone was shoved in front of her face. "Gloria wants to talk to you."

"No, thanks," Daisy said, batting the phone away.

"Daisy?" Gloria's voice came through, sounding far away. "If you don't talk to me, I'm coming over."

"I'm busy," Daisy shouted in the general direction of the phone. "Call back later." She took the phone from Lizzie and turned it off before tucking it under her again.

"Are you going to tell me what's going on?" Lizzie asked.

"No."

"Are you going to tell me why Colin Forsythe's looka-like has been camped out front for three days?"

"His name's Jamie and he's here because he's a jerk." She pulled another piece of dough from the bowl sitting on her stomach and began to roll it between her palms.

Lizzie sighed. "I'm worried about you."

"Don't worry about me." She stopped what she was doing to loll her head in Lizzie's direction. "Though you might want to think about looking for another job."

TWENTY-THREE MORE DAYS. The countdown was on. Daisy finished up the afternoon mixing and started pulling dough from the warmers. Yesterday had been rough, but she felt different today. It was just like the time she'd been dumped by her first real boyfriend in her sophomore year of high school.

There's nothing wrong with a good pity party, as long as it ends in a reasonable amount of time and you come back stronger than ever.

That's what her grandmother had said then and this morning, Daisy had woken up at 4:00 a.m. with Nana's voice in her head, saying the same thing. With renewed strength in her heart, she'd jumped out of bed and gone to work, even though Bruce was on the early shift this morning. If he was surprised by her presence, he didn't say anything.

Lizzie was another story.

"You might need drugs," she said when she saw Daisy working away in the kitchen. "It's nothing to be ashamed of—most of us need a little pharmaceutical intervention every now and then."

"I'm fine," Daisy insisted.

"No, you're not."

Taking Lizzie's hands, Daisy said, "Honestly. I'm fine." She forced a smile.

Lizzie narrowed her gaze. "Okay, if you're so fine, why don't you go deal with stalker dude?"

"Jamie's back?"

"He said he's not leaving until you talk to him."

Squaring her shoulders, Daisy said, "Fine. I'll talk to him."

She took two steps toward the door when Lizzie called, "Wait. Hairnet."

Daisy put a hand to her head. Her instinct to pull the net off, but she stopped herself. What did she care whether Jamie saw her in the horribly unattractive hairnet? It didn't matter. She didn't care what he thought. Except that there were other people out there, too, and Daisy did care about them, so she pulled the hairnet from her head at the last second and tucked it into her pocket.

The fact that her stomach somersaulted the moment she caught sight of Jamie was probably more a product of her stomach being empty than anything. It was an eighty per cent probability.

Okay, maybe sixty.

Forty-three.

She marched right up to the table where he was sitting and huffed what she hoped was a sound of exasperation.

Jamie responded with a cool, appraising gaze. His voice was deep and annoyingly calm. "Hey, Daisy. Why don't you join me?"

If only the man was a soft piece of dough that she could chuck at the ceiling. Or better yet, if only she had balls of dough to use as missiles. "You need to leave or I will call the police." There. That should do it. She tapped her foot.

Unfortunately, his lips curved up—not completely, but enough so that Daisy knew he was suppressing a smile.

"Call the police? What have I done?"

"You're loitering."

He shook his head, pointing at the numerous empty plates on his table. "I'm a paying customer. Today alone, I've sampled your cherry strudel, a cinnamon twist and three cheese buns. I'm not loitering."

Crossing her arms over her chest, Daisy countered, "You're harassing the staff."

"Harassing the staff?" Jamie leaned back in his chair, looking as if he was enjoying himself. Immensely.

Bastard!

"You mean the staff member who threatened me yesterday?"

"What? Who?"

"That one." He pointed at Lizzie. "She threatened to stab me." Jamie rubbed his chin in mock thoughtfulness. "Or maybe she was implying that you wanted to stab me. Either way, I was threatened."

Daisy groaned. "I don't want to stab you. Stabbing is too messy. We don't need Health and Safety all over us."

He might be able to keep his smile in check, but something that sounded suspiciously like a chuckle rattled around in that stupidly big chest of his. "That's what she said. Sounds like collusion to commit violence to me."

Daisy growled, her hands fisting at her sides. "God. I wish you were a bowl of dough."

"Why's that?"

"Because I'd like to punch you."

Jamie pushed his chair back and stood.

Stupid man. He did that on purpose so that she'd be forced to look up at him. Why was he so tall? It wasn't normal.

He spread his arms wide and said, "You want to have a go at me, go right ahead."

What was he trying to prove? "Is this entrapment?"

"No."

He patted his stomach, the washboard-like part of him that Daisy was all-too intimately familiar with.

"C'mon."

Daisy glanced around the busy bakery. "If you're trying to get me in trouble, I've already got enough of that."

"I'm not trying to get you in trouble."

"Then what is this?"

He took a step closer, so close that his appealing and unique scent wafted over her. Before she knew what she was doing, her eyes closed so she could focus on breathing him in, slowly and deeply.

She felt him bend down to her level, followed by the

tickle of her hair against her ear as he whispered, "Beating the shit out of someone can be very cathartic. However, it should be mutually agreed upon and done in a safe setting. Otherwise it's called assault and that's a felony." He paused, and Daisy heard him breathe in deeply, too. What was he doing? Smelling her?

Her stomach did a pole vault.

"Come back to my gym—no one will be there—and you can hit me as hard as you like. I give you permission to beat the crap out of me."

9

THIS WAS RIDICULOUS. What on earth was she doing here? She was seated on the counter in a men's locker room, surrounded by the aroma of pine-scented Lysol, mildew and sweat, wearing an old T-shirt and a pair of shorts that belonged to Jamie, while he wound athletic tape around her right hand.

She lifted her left shoulder to her nose and sniffed.

Fresh laundry and Jamie. Delicious.

No.

Not delicious. The clothes smelled good only because they'd been laundered and anything clean would, of course, smell divine in contrast to the stink of the locker room.

Daisy dropped her shoulder. For some reason she no longer felt angry. Was it Jamie's touch as he taped her hand? Or maybe it was the ride on his motorbike. Why was she such a sucker for a man with a motorcycle? She really had to figure that shit out because it was becoming dangerous.

"I know what you're thinking," she said to fill the troublesome silence.

"I doubt that."

Did he purposefully caress the inside of her wrist or

was that an accident? Daisy cleared her throat. "I'm not a violent woman."

Without looking up, Jamie said, "I didn't think you were."

"I've never hit anyone before in my life."

"All the more reason to hit me today."

She chewed on her lip. "Why are you doing this?"

He finished taping her right hand and then moved on to her left. "Two reasons."

When he didn't continue, Daisy asked, "Do you care to tell me what they are?"

Without looking up, he said, "You're angry with your situation and, therefore, me. You need to expel it so you can think clearly. This is the best way."

"I'm pretty sure most people would disagree with you." Daisy held her taped hand in front of her, wiggling her fingers, testing the limited movement.

"We'll see."

"What's the second reason?"

"All women should know how to defend themselves."

The seriousness of his tone made her flinch.

He caught her hand before she could tug it away. "Women are victims of violence way too often."

"So teach women to fight?"

"Why not?" Jamie resumed taping.

"It just seems like it's encouraging violence."

Jamie's chest rose and fell in a deep breath. Like he was angry or something. "That's the same argument people use for not teaching sex education in schools."

He held her hand in a fierce grip while softly caressing her fingertips. It was the strangest contradiction and it sent confused tingles up and down her spine.

"Knowledge is the best deterrent. Studies show informed young people make informed decisions. This is the same.

Women should know how to throw a punch. Where to hit. What it feels like. How not to be scared of it."

Jamie's gaze was so searing it took Daisy's breath away. It wasn't until he dropped his gaze that she was able to ask, "Do you know someone? Who's been the victim of violence, I mean?"

He was silent for so long, Daisy didn't think he was going to answer. But eventually he said, "I think we all do."

Blinking, she studied the top of Jamie's head as he continued to tape her hand. She tried to figure him out. This was the most serious she'd ever seen him, and while she hadn't known him long enough to see all his moods, this one took her by surprise. It was…stern. Protective.

Don't fall for it. It's all a trick, Daisy.

She let out a big breath—one she hadn't even realized she'd been holding—and shut her eyes, needing to focus on something other than the thickness of Jamie's hair and the gentle touch of his hands. Namely, conjuring up enough anger to hate him or, at the very least, hit him.

"There." He tore off the last strip of tape and proceeded to fit big, bulky gloves over her hands. He tightened the laces that ran up the inside of her palms and wrists. Once finished, lifted her down off the counter.

"Come on."

Daisy followed him out of the locker room, unsuccessfully trying to ignore the lingering sensation of his hands on her waist. In the main gym area, a ring was the central feature, spotlighted by the few lights Jamie had turned on. Surrounding the ring, Daisy could make out weight benches, barbells, pegboards, medicine balls and all kinds of bags hanging from the rafters, from big ones to small, teardrop-shaped ones. Jamie moved a stool over to the edge of the ring so she could climb up, and then he separated the ropes so she was able to crawl between them easily.

While Jamie stood in the center, waiting for her, she wandered around the perimeter, her stomach in knots, pretending to check out the rest of the gym. This had to be one of the craziest things she'd done. Ever.

"Where is everyone?"

"We're closed Fridays."

"Oh." She made her way to the center of the ring. "So, now what?"

He opened his arms wide. "Now you hit me."

"This is stupid."

"Why?"

"It just feels weird."

He sauntered up to her. "Hit me."

The crazy desire to inflict pain had vanished. In fact, the only crazy desire she had left was to touch Jamie's skin. And that wasn't happening. Ever again.

Nope.

"C'mon."

"Fine." She lifted a fist and bopped Jamie on the shoulder with the fat part of the glove.

He made a face. "You can do better than that."

She shoved him with both hands.

"Really?"

"What?"

"Worse than I thought."

"I told you, I'm not a fighter…" That was the end of the sentence and yet her words trailed off as if it wasn't.

Jamie's gaze met hers, a single brow raised. The first part of *I'm a lover, not a fighter* echoed silently between them.

"Right," Jamie said, clearing the air. "Let's start with your stance." He looked her up and down and then, without warning, shoved her.

"Hey!" He hadn't pushed her hard, but it was enough to make her stumble back a couple of steps.

"You're off balance." He demonstrated how to stand: legs spread, knees bent, hands up. "Try this."

Daisy copied his stance, or thought she did, but by the shake of his head, she could tell Jamie didn't think so. He walked around behind her and nudged her left foot with his toe. "You want this toe to point at your opponent." Then he gently kicked her right foot a little farther out. "Shoulder-width and turned out more. Not too square."

"Okay."

"Now lift your right heel so you're on the ball of your foot." He wandered in front of her. "This is so you can move quickly." He demonstrated the stance and the quick movements it allowed.

"Um, okay."

Facing her, he assessed her with narrowed eyes. Up and down. Up and...pause, then down. Why did his gaze make her pulse race? Was it the overhead lights that heated her skin?

"Bend your knees. Yes. Good. Now, think of yourself as buoyant, floating." He demonstrated the movement—quick bobs—and Daisy tried to mimic it but had no idea if she was successful or not.

She stopped moving when he walked around behind her again and rested his hands on her hips. In fact, all her thoughts ceased completely as her olfactory senses took over. Daisy sniffed. Jamie smelled freshly laundered—the same scent as the clothes she was wearing.

Nice.

"Relax your hips." He gently swiveled her hips back and forth. "Relax."

Yeah, not happening. Not when his hands were on her, moving her in some weird reverse slow dance. It only got worse when he reached around to her chin and gently tugged on it. "Chin down." While still behind her, he slid his hands to her shoulders. "Relax your shoulders."

She closed her eyes.

"You're going to keep your left hand here. Your right goes here." His big hands slid down as though he was hugging her from behind.

Flashes of last Saturday night—Jamie behind her, holding her, one hand on her shoulder, the other arm wrapped around her waist, thrusting—

"Elbows in."

Daisy's lips parted as she panted. This did not feel natural. Not one bit. Not with Jamie's big body pressed up against her back, his hands adjusting her, the freshly laundered scent of him. Oh, God. She was having a hard time catching her breath.

"Good." He moved around in front of her and shoved. Though she still wasn't prepared, this time she didn't move.

"There. You see?"

No, Daisy did not see. All she could do at the moment was feel. Jamie's hands lingering on her—her hips, her shoulders, her chin, her arms, touching her, kissing her, undressing her...

"Daisy?"

"Hmm?"

"I'm going to teach you how to jab now."

"To jab?"

"Yes. It's the first punch beginners learn...ah, Daisy?"

"Mmm-hmm."

"You have to open your eyes."

"Oh!"

Jamie's eyes sparkled as if he knew exactly what she had been thinking about. He managed to work his expression into something vaguely resembling seriousness as he positioned himself in his stance. "It's a quick movement with your hand. Okay? You're going to lift your shoulder…" He demonstrated the movement. "Rotate your arm and…jab!" His hand whipped out, his fist flying at her, so close that she let out a little shriek, releasing her from the spell he'd cast.

With a grin he said, "Okay. Your turn."

MAYBE BOXING REALLY wasn't Daisy's thing. Just because so many of the people he knew had joined the club—men, anyway—didn't mean it was for everyone. Whenever he tried to give her instruction, her eyes glazed over, her responses were slow and hesitant and she continually asked him to repeat himself, as if he spoke a different language.

And she was breathing heavily, like this was a real workout for her.

"No, that's a cross. For a hook you want to…"

Daisy dropped her gloved hands to her sides and blinked. "I'm done."

"You haven't even hit me yet."

"Sure I have. I've hit you tons." She motioned toward his outfacing palms, which she'd been using as targets.

"It's not the same. You said you wanted to punch me. You've got to punch me."

She shook her head, and her hair curled around her shoulders. God, he loved her hair, the way her curls were a natural extension of her bubbly, fun, unexpected personality, bouncing all over the place. Soft to the touch. Just enough to grip when he needed to.

"I don't feel like it anymore."

Jamie stood in front of her, considering the situation, knowing what he needed to do but uncertain whether it was wise.

Daisy lifted her wrists toward him. "Untie me and take me back, please."

Oh, God. He had a vision of her—wrists tied together with one of his ties, for Pete's sake—asking the very same question, kneeling on a bed…naked.

Without thinking he tore off his shirt. Daisy's wide-eyed expression provided some gratification, but that wasn't what he was going for. He spread his arms, widened his stance and said, "Hit me." Patting his stomach, he prompted, "Right here."

She shook her head.

By God, that hair would be the death of him.

He took small, sliding steps back and forth in front of her. "Hit me for lying to you."

Her gaze narrowed.

"Hit me for being a man." He patted his stomach again.

The shakes of her head became shorter. Tighter.

"Hit me for representing your ex-husband."

Her lips worked angrily against one another. Chewing, pressing, snarling. She was close. So close.

He stopped moving, met her cloudy gaze and said softly, "Hit me for all the years. All the hard work. For all you're about to lose. Hit me for Nana Sin's."

The sound Daisy made was like an animal caught in a trap. Keening. Angry. Hurt. Desperate. She flew at him, her hands flying, punches landing on his chest, his stomach, his shoulders and jaw. A few of them even had some power behind them.

Jamie relaxed his hips and sank into his stance, absorbing it all, taking it, not defending himself, not blocking a single punch.

He thought her cries of anger might turn into sobs as she worked herself into exhaustion, but he was wrong. She became more feral, her punches quicker. Her jabs pretty good for a beginner.

"Why did you tell Alan you didn't know me?" she cried.

His natural inclination was to dance out of the way of her flying fists, but he stood his ground. "I had to."

"Why?"

"We'd just slept together." Her fist found the corner of his jaw. "Ouch. Nice one." He worked his jaw back and forth before answering. "It's a conflict of interest."

"So drop him." She landed a hard right hook, the very punch he didn't think she'd paid enough attention to to learn.

"Alan's entitled to more than he's asking for." He dodged her fist so he could finish speaking. "Other lawyers might try harder to convince him to go for more. I won't do that."

His dodge threw her off balance, angering her.

"Oomph." He let out a burst of air from the unexpected knee to his gut.

"Why?" she shouted. "Why would you do that?"

"Why do you think?" he said, panting, bent over from the temporary loss of breath.

He was fully prepared for more abuse when he straightened, but Daisy didn't continue her onslaught. She simply stared at him, her pretty lips working. With a snarl, she lifted her wrist to her mouth, caught the laces between her teeth and tugged, loosening the ties enough so that when she wedged the glove between her knees, she was able to pull her hand out.

"What are you doing?"

She grunted as she grappled with the laces on the other glove, loosening them.

"Daisy, you don't want to hit me without gloves. It'll hurt and…"

"I'm not going to hit you, dum-dum," Daisy snapped. The other glove dropped at her feet. She shoved him much like he'd done to her earlier.

Jamie didn't budge.

This seemed to anger her or…something. Because she body-checked him. He grabbed her shoulders and squeezed. "What are you doing?"

"I don't know." She gazed up at him, her face flushed from the frenzy, her lips parted and moist. "I need… something."

"What?"

"I don't know!" She howled in frustration. Using all her body weight, she shoulder-checked him, grunting. But instead of letting him stumble back, she grabbed for him, her fingers curling around the waistband of his shorts. She blinked up at him, nostrils flared, fingertips dipping cautiously beneath the elastic, brushing the skin of his abdomen.

"Daisy?"

"Do something."

Oh, God. She had to stop looking at him like that. The angry need, her mouth open and inviting. So kissable. He swiped his thumb across her lower lip. She should have turned away. She didn't.

No, what she did was reckless and seductive: she opened her mouth and sucked him in.

Oh, hell, no. He withdrew his thumb, slowly.

She blinked up at him. "Do it."

He shook his head.

"Kiss me."

He tried to back away, but she had a vise grip on his shorts.

"Please."

Shit.

He fit his fingers through her hair and held her face. Before he could stop himself, he leaned down and took her mouth in the way he'd wanted to all day. Just like his words and taunts had activated her anger, his kiss activated her passion. She would have devoured him if he wasn't already devouring her. While their lips were locked, she struggled out of his too-big shirt, wrenching herself away from his kiss only long enough to snatch the shirt off.

His hands went to her breasts. So lush, so feminine, so beautiful. He groaned into her mouth and she replied with the sexiest little moan. Seriously, this woman. "Daisy…?"

"Shh." She silenced him with a deep kiss, exploring his mouth before trailing her lips across his jaw and down his neck. A part of him—a very small part of him—knew this was mad and he should stop. But that would take someone noble, and there was not one noble bone in his body at the moment.

While her kisses moved from his throat to his chest, she reached lower, covering his arousal with her small hand.

That was it.

He was done.

With a groan he unsnapped her bra, lifted her up and took a nipple into his mouth. He was not gentle. He couldn't be gentle if he tried. Daisy brought out a savage need in him. He had to have her. He had to feel her body beneath his, skin to skin. Her moans a product of his actions. Her passion brought on by his need.

They fell together, Jamie taking the brunt of the impact as Daisy rolled on top of him. He quickly rectified the situation by rolling her over. The exertion of their boxing bout had only made her tastier—her skin sweet and salty, a delicious combination. Jamie had to sample all of her. He kissed her mouth, her ear, beneath her jaw and throat, his kisses bordering on bites. Sucking a tender bit of skin inside his mouth, he wasn't satisfied until he heard Daisy moan, until she arched beneath him and her fingernails dug into his back.

So good.

He needed more. He always needed more with her. While his mouth found her sweet, sweet breast, his hands found their way beneath the sagging shorts. His shorts.

Why was it a turn-on to see a woman wearing his clothes? He didn't know. Except now that he had, he wanted her out of them.

Right now.

"Jamie."

His name, spoken on a sigh, had to be the best sound. He sank his hand deeper inside the shorts, sliding his fingers over her satiny panties that would no doubt match the pretty bra she wore.

"Oh, God."

He glanced up from where he was positioned, his face on a level with her sweetly indented navel. "Do you want me to stop?"

With eyes half-closed, she lolled her head back and forth across the ring floor.

"Daisy, look at me."

She opened her eyes.

"Say the words. I need to hear you say them."

She blinked to focus, though the haze remained. "Don't stop, Jamie. Please. Don't stop."

10

WHILE PUNCHING JAMIE was cathartic, this was so much better.

Why did it feel so good? Jamie's hands on her hips, his lips on her belly. Kissing, nibbling, tasting, while his hand stroked beneath the shorts. It was so good. Deliciously good.

Painfully good.

She tried to roll away when his kisses approached the waistband of the shorts, but his hold was too strong.

"Too late. You're not going anywhere," he growled.

"Jamie." She both wanted him to stop and lifted her hips in encouragement.

What was wrong with her?

She had no idea, but she needed to get her shorts off, pronto, because she was sure that would make her feel better. She fit her hands beneath the waistbands of her shorts and panties and pushed, wriggling her ass to get them off. Jamie helped, yanking them from her ankles and moving between her parted legs.

He bit the inside of her bare thigh. It was exquisite.

"More," she begged.

His hands preceded his lips, sliding roughly up her

thighs, squeezing her flesh as he moved higher and higher. "Is this what you want?" He flicked her clit with his tongue.

"Yes."

He groaned, spread her and dropped his mouth to kiss her in the most intimate way imaginable.

"Oh!" The sensation of his mouth on her was so sudden and stirring that her eyes popped open. The sight of Jamie's thick hair against her belly, his strong hands gripping her, while he lay shirtless between her parted legs only added to the over-the-top stimuli of his mouth, teeth and tongue.

Her body bucked beneath his as his kisses became more aggressive, and she needed something for her hands to give her purchase. There was nothing except his hair to hold on to.

Jamie's head lifted, his eyes smoldering behind half-shut lids. He licked his lips. "I'm going to make you come. You okay with that?"

"Jamie, I need..."

He bent back to her, touching his tongue to her clit. Her body quaked in response, making Daisy forget what she was about to say. The very next second he lapped along her warmth, and she gave herself over to the sensations of his mouth and hands because there was nothing else she could do. She threw her head back, loving the tickle of his hair against the sensitive skin of her thigh, giving in to his firm grasp, allowing him to spread her open for his pleasure.

"Ah!"

When he plunged a finger inside of her, it was like something red and hot pierced her, reaching all the way through her belly to her throat, bending her like a bow, right off the floor. It was all so much: the pounding of her blood through her veins, the feel of his mouth on such an intimate part of her, the sensation of his fingers moving in and out at the same time as his tongue, claiming her together, taking what he wanted just like he'd allowed her to take out her anger on him.

And then...holy hell!

Orgasm hit her like an unexpected cross after a fury of jabs, the fierce explosion taking her completely unaware, making her scream and yank on Jamie's hair to keep from flying off the floor in ecstasy.

How did he do it? How had he brought her there so quickly? So thoroughly? It was...

Daisy didn't know what it was, but it kept going and going.

How long was it before she opened her eyes? Seconds? Minutes? Hours?

Jamie's face came into view and she blinked, trying to focus on his smile. So seductive. Knowing. Tender.

"How are you feeling?" He brushed a hand across her forehead, smoothing hair out of her eyes.

"Good." She bit her lip but released it as Jamie leaned down to kiss her softly. Wow, the man could kiss. His lips were warm and soft. Gentle. These lips that had just made love to another part of her now sweetly made love to her mouth.

Too soon he stopped, but he remained propped above her, looking down at her with warmth in his chocolate eyes. He reached past her head and grabbed her shirt, passing it to her. "Get dressed. We need to talk."

She frowned and pushed herself into a sitting position. It wasn't until she was upright that the gravity of what had just happened descended upon her. She was sitting—naked—in a boxing ring, of all places. She glanced down at her nakedness.

Dear God.

She'd just let Jamie... Shit!

Daisy hurriedly pulled the shirt on, not bothering with

her bra. Finding her panties beneath her, she yanked them on. All the aggression and passion of earlier had passed, leaving only one thing in its wake.

"You okay?" Jamie asked as he helped her through the ropes.

"Yep."

"Because you're acting like you're not okay."

"I'm fine. Just need a quick shower." She forced a smile and hurried to the locker room. Her appearance in the full-length mirror inside the door stopped her. Her hair was clumpy and messy, sticking to her neck in places and sticking out haphazardly in others.

Sex hair.

Her cheeks were flushed.

Sex cheeks.

Her lips swollen.

Sex…

"Quiet," she whispered to her reflection. "I know what I did. You can be quiet now." She scrubbed a hand up and down her face. This was a disaster. She was a disaster.

She'd come to the gym to make herself feel better and instead she felt worse. So much worse. Daisy dropped her clothes on the floor, turned on the shower and stepped under the hot spray, using the soap dispenser on the wall to wash as quickly as she could.

How could she?

Falling against the cool tiles of the shower stall, Daisy lifted her face to the spray. It was completely possible that some of the moisture streaming down her cheeks was of her own making, because Daisy had never been in a lower place in her life.

It was bad enough that Alan had betrayed her by cheating, leaving her and then demanding half the bakery. Then there was her mother: her betrayal had started from the moment Daisy was born.

But she was the worst, the very worst betrayer of them all, because she'd betrayed herself. How could she give in to lust and stupid physical desire when her very happiness and livelihood were on the line? How could she?

Now she had absolutely nothing left. Not even her self-esteem.

If only she could blame Jamie.

Banging her head against the tile, Daisy didn't want to think of Jamie. Whenever she thought of him, things went sideways. Take what happened in the ring, for example. It wasn't Jamie's fault. *She* was the one who jumped him, asking him to kiss her.

He'd even given her a chance to stop. *Say the words. I need to hear you say them.*

Had she taken the out?

Nope.

Her response?

Don't stop, Jamie. Good lord! She'd begged him.

She had to get out of there. No more Jamie. No more crazy physical attraction to a man who was helping destroy her.

Definitely no more sex.

She turned the shower off and squeezed the water from her hair. Clean towels were stacked on a shelf outside the showers and Daisy dried off, her hands shaking, making getting dressed in a hurry difficult. Once she was ready, she slung her bag over her shoulder and marched out of the locker room and into the gym, where Jamie was waiting for her. She pressed his now folded but still-damp clothes against his chest and kept walking.

"Where are you going?" he asked.

"Back to the bakery."

"We need to talk, Daisy," he said, following her. "We can do it here or back there, but I'm not letting you go until we've talked."

"We have nothing to say to one another." She looked up at him. Mistake. Her stomach did a mutinous flippity-flop at the sight of him. Face still flushed, hair in disarray from *her* fingers, lips still swollen…

Sex lips.

Oh, God. She gave her head a shake. This was wrong. So wrong.

"Are you still working for Alan?"

He hesitated. "Yes."

"Then I have nothing to say to you."

"Daisy. We just—"

She spun on him. "We just what? You let me punch you. I let you…kiss me." She pointed to her jeans, ignoring the flash of anger that sparked in Jamie's eyes. "It was physical. Nothing more."

She walked out the door on noodley legs, wondering if they were going to join her stomach in the mutiny against her, as well. Much to her surprise, they supported her all the way down the steps to the curb, where she was able to flag down a cab.

"Daisy," Jamie called as she pulled open the door to the car. "This isn't over."

"Yes. Oh, yes, it is."

DAISY EMPTIED THE remaining wine into her glass. "I hope you brought another bottle. I'm all out."

Gloria took Daisy's glass and poured half of the wine into her own glass. "Getting drunk is not the answer."

"Are you kidding? It's an absolute necessity in this case." And it was, for so many reasons. She needed to forget about her divorce, about the impossible situation she was in…

about Jamie. Yes, Jamie was the worst part of it all because even though the situation with the divorce was dire, it was Jamie who occupied her thoughts and yesterday with him in the gym had only made things worse. Even now, she could feel the ghost of his hands on her, the whisper of his lips and tongue...

Gloria studied her. "So, let me get this straight, Colin Forsythe's brother is representing Alan."

"Yep."

"And it was him, not Colin, who came to the bakery to interview you for the article?"

"Yep."

"So did something happen between the two of you?" Gloria leaned toward her, expectantly.

Daisy dismissed the question with a wave. "You're getting off track."

"Okay," Gloria said slowly, indicating to Daisy that questions about Jamie would likely resume at a later date. "So, how much time do you have before the bank takes the bakery?"

"Huh?" Daisy swallowed a big gulp of wine. It wasn't having the numbing effect she'd hoped it would have by now. "Oh, um...twenty-two days."

"Daisy!" Gloria sat up straight. "Tell me you're joking."

"Nope."

"Why haven't you said something? Why did you leave it so long?"

"I don't know. I thought maybe a miracle would happen, you know?"

Gloria raised the glass to her mouth. "So, what are we talking here?"

"I need to pay Alan seven hundred fifty thousand."

"Dollars?"

"No, tiddlywinks. Of course, dollars."

Wine dribbled out of Gloria's glass where she'd tipped it toward her mouth but didn't drink when she heard the sum. "Seven hundred and fifty G? Are you kidding me?"

"Wish I was."

"Daisy."

"I know." Daisy swallowed the remainder of the wine.

"Have you talked to your mother? Her boyfriend's loaded, isn't he? Maybe they'll help you out."

"I tried. Do you know what she said?"

Gloria shook her head.

"It'd be good for me to let Nana Sin's go."

"Hmm." Setting her glass down, Gloria went to find a cloth beside Daisy's sink and returned to wipe up the spilled wine. "What about a loan, a second mortgage?"

"I don't qualify."

"How is that possible?" Gloria spread her arms. "You own the whole building. What about the equity?"

Twisting the stem of her wine glass, Daisy said, "I already took out a line of credit for the repairs and the renovation. Just in my name. The rest is basically Alan's. According to the bank."

"Daisy!"

The pressure inside her made it difficult to speak. She'd left it too long. She'd acted like nothing was wrong, compartmentalized everything so well. Now that the time was here, she couldn't believe it. It wasn't real. It couldn't be real.

"A payment plan?"

"Alan offered that in the beginning but I was angry. Hurt."

Tapping her fingernails against the counter top, Gloria asked, "Is he still seeing *that woman*?"

Daisy shrugged. "I don't know." That was another thing Daisy chose not to think about, though the burning ache in her stomach reminded her of how hurt she'd been when he'd told her. The memory of that night crashed through her thoughts like Godzilla in the streets of Tokyo.

I'm seeing someone else.

She makes time for me, and she makes me feel special.

I'm leaving and I want my share of the estate.

This was all a win-win for Alan: seven hundred fifty thousand dollars that didn't belong to him and a new, prettier woman while Daisy got screwed, and not in the good way.

Standing, Gloria set her glass down. "Okay, we can figure this out." She paced the short length of Daisy's kitchen. "You need to come up with money, fast." Daisy had seen Gloria like this before. When presented with a problem, her tiny redheaded friend could not sit still until it was solved. Daisy reached for Gloria's wineglass and drank while watching her friend think.

"You don't have much time." The conversation didn't require answers. Gloria was having the conversation all on her own. "Lots of money, little time." Gloria stopped, her eyes blazing. "A fund-raiser."

Daisy shook her head. "We can't do that."

"Why not?"

"I'm not a charity."

"That doesn't matter." Gloria's eyes blazed. "Crowd-funding."

"What's that?"

"It's a way to raise money online. People do it to raise capital for all sorts of projects—to start up businesses, for hard times, college fees, litigation fees. It's perfect for you. Nana Sin's is a Chicago treasure. That's even what the article said in the *Tribune*." She pounded the counter top. "We can do it, Daisy. We'll have a big party here with celebrities and the media. We'll have a group here doing stuff online, like a telethon, except they won't be answering phones. They'll be posting to the internet." She waved her hands in the air. "Save Nana Sin's!"

"But…"

"No buts." Gloria snatched the wineglass from Daisy's hand and finished the sip that was left. "Don't you worry. I'll take care of everything."

Jamie had to stay away from Daisy Sinclair. That much was clear. He was jeopardizing his client, the firm and his career. Not to mention his sanity. He'd invited her to the gym only to try and help in the best way he knew how. Hadn't he started the boxing club after one of the most traumatic events of his life? It was therapeutic, and he wasn't the only one who used the ring to exorcise his demons. That was what he'd tried to do for Daisy.

Except that when he let Daisy take her angst out on him, she'd awoken a beast, and he'd become the very thing he loathed, the kind of man who took advantage of a woman when she was down. All she'd had to do was gaze up at him with that mixture of innocence and sensuality and he was lost. All she had to do was ask, and he'd do whatever she wanted. Right or wrong.

And what he'd done with Daisy in the ring was wrong.

His life was a holy mess, and Carson's desertion of the firm only made things worse. He'd called last night and said he was leaving the practice altogether.

"How can you do this?" Jamie had said, unable to comprehend. "It's insane."

"I'm in love. What can I say?"

"You can say this is all a big joke."

"Nope. I never thought it'd happen to me, but it did, and I'm going to set up a practice for inheritance planning here in Florida."

"Wills? You're doing wills? You'll die of boredom."

"Bored? Are you kidding me? I'm finally living. I bought a boat. I'll work mornings, spend the afternoon fishing." Connor laughed, not the sardonic laugh Jamie was accustomed to from him, but a lighthearted chuckle. "In the evenings I will make love to my beautiful wife—"

"Okay, okay. I get the picture."

That was Friday, right after he'd returned from the gym. Right after he'd been with Daisy and she'd walked out on him before he'd had a chance to talk things through with her. The sour sensation in his gut hadn't let up since, and he'd been popping antacid like candy even though it didn't give him any relief.

Sitting at his desk now, he stared dejectedly at the massive pile in his inbox and set about prioritizing files when Helen knocked then stuck her head inside his door. "Jamie, there's a client here to see you."

"I don't have any appointments booked."

"She's new."

"Helen, I'm overloaded. I can't take any new clients right now."

"She's insistent."

Pinching the bridge of his nose, Jamie rose from his desk and opened his office door. An attractive redhead stood just outside. Her eyes widened when she saw him.

"Wow. You two really are identical. Poor Daisy."

"I'm sorry. Who are you?"

She motioned toward his office. When he opened the door wider, she strode right on in. After he closed the door behind her she said, "I'm Gloria. Daisy's best friend."

"Did Daisy send you?"

"No. She doesn't know I'm here."

"Do you need advice about a divorce?"

She laughed. "Oh, no. Nothing like that."

"Then why are you here?"

She made a face that involved pursing her lips and rolling her eyes. "I need your help. Actually, I need Colin's help, but I thought I'd come to you first."

"Why?"

"Because I wanted to meet you. Daisy was a little vague."

Jamie tamped down the desire to ask what Daisy had said about him. Though he probably didn't want to know as it was likely derogatory.

"Anyway, you and your brother owe Daisy, and right now I'm collecting from everyone who owes her. Believe me, the list is long."

11

WHERE HAD THE past twenty days gone? Daisy had thrown herself into working every shift at the bakery—giving her no time to think about money, her ex, or Jamie and how she hadn't heard from him since the gym—and now, here it was, the night before the big fund-raiser. The bakery was closed, but that didn't mean it was quiet. There was a horde of party planners streaming in and out, decorating the place with balloons and banners that read Save Nana Sin's.

Daisy had tried to help but found she was just getting in the way, so now she sat in a corner of the kitchen, watching the mayhem like an outsider.

"There you are," Gloria said, bustling in with bags under her arms. "Everything okay?"

"Fine."

Gloria was followed by a man carrying a huge box. "That can go in the office at the back." She pointed the way to the door and then sat down beside Daisy, plopping the bags on the butcher block. "God, this is fun, isn't it?"

"Mmm…" Daisy tried to share in her friend's enthusiasm but was unable to do it. The fear of failure was just too strong. Instead of answering, she asked, "So, what's in the box?"

"T-shirts." Gloria reached inside a bag, pulling one out. "They're supercute." She held it up. The shirt had a caricature of an angel holding a doughnut with a big bite taken out of it. The caption read Heavenly! At the bottom was the Nana Sin's logo. Then Gloria showed her the back, where there was a caricature of a devil devouring a doughnut—crumbs flying—with the words, Sinfully Delicious. Don't Even Try to Resist.

Daisy reached for the shirt. It was cute. "Are we wearing these?"

"Yep. I've got one for all of our celebrity guests and staff. But they're also for donors." From her bag she pulled out her tablet, tapped it and showed the screen to Daisy. "I set you up on GoFundMe. The way it works is that people who donate less than fifty dollars get an e-copy of your cinnamon bun recipe. Donate between fifty and one hundred and they get the recipe *and* a T-shirt."

"Wait, are there enough T-shirts in that box?"

"No, silly. We don't send them out." She tapped the screen to show Daisy the website of a T-shirt company. "They're sent direct from the distributor. Saves on shipping, and the more that end up being ordered, the lower the cost per shirt and the more we raise!"

Daisy shook her head. How on earth did her friend know all this stuff?

Flipping back to the GoFundMe page, Gloria said, "Anything over one hundred is the T-shirt, the recipe and something *special*."

"What?"

Gloria craned her head in the direction of the door.

"What are you doing?"

"Where are they? They were right behind me."

"Who?"

A moment later, Daisy's mother and Alexander came

in. Cynthia was looking like her normal self, completely put together in a way that appeared as if she hadn't spent a second on her makeup when Daisy knew it was at least a forty-five-minute production to achieve that natural, flawless look.

"Wow. It's a zoo out there."

Daisy stood. "What are you two doing here?"

"Didn't Gloria tell you?" Cynthia asked.

Daisy shook her head.

Gloria scurried around the counter, giving Cynthia a hug and a peck on the cheek. "I wanted you to be here when I showed her."

What was going on? Why was her best friend sharing a secretive smile with her mother? That was *not* normal.

Gloria tapped on the screen of her tablet and then put the tablet on the counter for all to see. There was an image of a generous cinnamon bun on a plate surrounded by other baked goods. The presentation was lovely and the image made Daisy's mouth water. The type read, "Nana Sin's Secret Recipes."

"What is this?" Daisy asked.

"*This* is the something special." Gloria's grin was so wide she was in danger of splitting her face open. "Swipe."

Daisy swiped the tablet. Next was a copyright page, followed by a table of contents that included a foreword, "Secrets to the Most 'Sinfully' Delicious Baking," with tips and tricks for preparing dough and pastry, and then the heading, "Nana Sin's Secret Recipes," followed by an alphabetized list of recipes. Daisy tapped on the recipe section and started swiping. There was page after page of *her* recipes accompanied by gorgeous images of *her* baking.

"A recipe book?"

"A recipe *e-book*," Gloria corrected her.

"We didn't have time for print books," her mom said.

"But…how did you even have time for this?" she asked as she kept swiping through the recipes. "Who took these pictures?"

"Those are mine," Gloria explained. "I've been taking pictures of your baking forever. Posting all that yummy stuff to Instagram. Then I matched up the pictures with the recipes you gave me. Lizzie helped."

Daisy went back to the table of contents. "What about the foreword?" She clicked on it. "Who wrote this?"

"I did," Cynthia said cautiously.

Daisy read a passage on dough preparation. It was good. Really good. "But how do you know all this?"

Indicating the bakery with a sweep of her hand, Cynthia said, "Don't forget I grew up here, too. Your grandmother taught me everything. Or tried to."

Daisy swiped through the recipes one more time. "Wow, you guys. This is amazing. How do we distribute this?"

Alex stepped closer. "Barkley Adams did the editing—he's that publisher friend of mine—"

"The one who contracted me to write my book," Cynthia added.

"He recommended we go through his publishing house. They've got us set up on all e-retailers: Amazon, iTunes, Barnes and Noble. They'll do a free promo code for those who donate a certain amount."

Daisy bobbed her head, though as far as she was concerned, Alex was speaking gibberish.

"So?" Gloria asked. "What do you think?"

"What do I think? I'm blown away by all this." Daisy's voice caught when she read the dedication, *For Nana.* "Thank you. Thank you so much."

Daisy's mother smiled wide—gosh, she really was a beautiful woman—while Alex wrapped an arm around her, squeezing her close. "It was the least we could do for you, Daisy. I only wish we could do more."

"Well, if you wouldn't mind helping out tomorrow, that would be great."

"We wouldn't miss it," Cynthia said with an uncharacteristic amount of enthusiasm.

Daisy wanted to believe that her mother's intentions were good, but years of history told her that she wasn't doing this for Daisy—she was doing it for herself. The question was, why?

For the first time in a long time, Daisy felt...hopeful.

She marveled at the sheer volume of people crowded into Nana Sin's, at the organized chaos. How had Gloria done it? The woman was not only the best of best friends, she had a talent for fund-raising. Or crowdfunding. Or whatever the hell this was.

There were people camped out in her office, all on computers, doing who-the-hell-knew-what. There was extra help in the kitchen, even though both Daisy and Bruce had been up in the wee hours of the morning, tripling all the recipes. And out in the front? Well, it was mayhem.

Absolute mayhem.

Reporters. Cameras. People, people, people. So many people they'd set up tables on the sidewalk outside. Gloria was in her element: flitting from person to person, smiling and laughing, cheeks glowing, eyes sparkling, taking endless selfies. She loved this shit. For the split second that Daisy stood there, unnoticed and holding a tray of baked goods, she grinned, filled with the sheer love and joy of it all.

Then she saw Jamie and her joy turned to turmoil. Sidling up to Gloria, she whispered, "What is *he* doing here?"

Gloria turned. "Colin Forsythe? He's the new cohost of *The Chicago Gourmet*. They're doing a special on you."

"Oh, that's Colin." How could she still confuse the two?

"Yep." Gloria waved him over. "He's been very helpful. So has Jamie." Gloria gave her a meaningful look.

"Jamie?" Daisy's tummy did a nose-dive. "He's not here is he?"

"Haven't seen him," Gloria said, though her attention was on a woman with a microphone on the other side of the room. "Oh, look, there's W7 News. I'll be right back."

Gloria took off just as Colin made his way over. While he was the same height as Jamie, his hair was still shorter, his nose straighter. Now that he was close, Daisy noticed his eyes were a lighter shade of brown. More of a milk chocolate to Jamie's rich, dark chocolate. Strange.

"Daisy. I need to apologize."

She shook her head. "No need."

"I hope my brother explained sufficiently." He glanced back at his cohost, Tricia Gordon.

"Honestly, he didn't explain at all. But he did apologize." *The ass.* From the peculiar look Colin gave her, Daisy couldn't be sure whether the last bit was said in her head or accidentally out loud.

"Good." He cleared his throat. "I'd like to make it up to you. Today."

"Thank you." She raised the tray and offered him a cinnamon bun. He took the bun, smiled, bit into it, and frowned. "It's good."

Odd. His expression said the opposite. He took another bite that he didn't seem to enjoy before being called off to tape a short interview with one of her regular customers.

There was another difference between the brothers. For all that Colin was the food critic, Jamie had been so much more expressive and appreciative of her cinnamon bun.

Maybe Colin just didn't like sweets. Boy, things sure would have been different if it had really been Colin who'd come to do the review of Nana Sin's instead of Jamie.

Would he have been as complimentary in his review? She doubted it. She also doubted he would have flirted with her, and he certainly wouldn't have asked her out on a date.

And of course, Daisy wouldn't have slept with him—that went without saying.

Thank God it was Jamie who came, who saw her in her underwear, who asked her out and made her feel feminine and womanly and wonderful.

"Ouch!"

Someone stepped on her toe, and Daisy nearly dropped the tray.

"Sorry about that, darlin'." Daisy turned to find the biggest cowboy she'd ever seen—not that she'd seen many cowboys walking around the streets of Chicago—smiling down at her. "You must be Daisy."

"Hi." She offered him the tray because she didn't know what else to do.

"Don't mind if I do, though this is my third one." He put a finger to his lips. "Don't tell." Gesturing with his chin, he indicated Gloria, who was still being interviewed by the news team. "She's already given me hell for eating more than my share." His eyes twinkled as he demolished half the bun in one bite. The expression on the cowboy's face after tasting the bun was one of appreciation. "Damn, that's good." He grinned at her and moved on so that others could snatch a bun from the tray. It was like a stampede, and in seconds, every last bun had disappeared.

As the circle of men dispersed, Gloria made her way back over, smiling widely.

"Where did you find all these people?" Daisy asked. "And by people, I mean enormously large men?" She hadn't noticed until this very second that ninety percent of the crowd consisted of large, muscle-bound men.

"It's good, right?" Gloria gestured to the mass. "For marketing purposes, who do people want to see eating Nana Sin's baking? Women want to see hot, muscular guys, and guys want to see their favorite athletes. So, we've got football players, hockey players… There's some kind of pro bull-riding thingamajig going on right now, hence all the cowboy hats."

"You're amazing."

"This—" Gloria waved her hand at the masses "—was not my idea or my doing. But I'm loving it." The smile fell away from her face as she stared across the room. "Who is that Neanderthal?"

"Who?"

"The big one with the cowboy hat. I'm going to kill him." Gloria pushed her way through the crowd and strode directly up to the cowboy who'd just stepped on Daisy's foot. Even from a distance she could tell that Gloria was letting him have it by the way her hip was sticking out and her hands were flying out of control. The cowboy didn't budge; in fact, he almost seemed to grow taller as she yelled at him for whatever sin he'd committed.

Daisy grinned. God, she was so lucky to have a friend like Gloria.

"Ten thousand." Someone called out.

"What does that mean?" Daisy asked a young man who was tapping away on his cell phone.

"That's how much we've raised so far."

Daisy checked her watch. "It's only been half an hour."

"Just wait. It'll snowball from here," the guy said.

Daisy felt lightheaded. She wanted to ask Gloria more questions, but Gloria was still giving the cowboy hell, and Daisy didn't want to interrupt the fun. Looking panicked by the mob of people, her assistant baker, Bruce, pushed his way to Daisy's side. He passed her a tray full of strudel, muttering, "You're the face of Nana Sin's. You take it." Then he grabbed the empty tray and disappeared again through the throng into the back.

Bruce was a wonderful baker, but not much for customer service.

Within seconds, Daisy was surrounded.

"I'll have one of those."

"Save one for me."

"What is this? It's so friggin' good."

Daisy was murmuring her thanks to all the celebrity guests when she felt someone standing close behind her. Then she caught his scent, unique to one man, and she closed her eyes to inhale deeply.

"Hi, Daisy. I like your T-shirt." Was he purposefully speaking to her in a low, seductive voice, or was that just the way he always spoke?

Well, she wasn't going to let on that his voice had any effect on her. Nope. She turned, adopting Gloria's stance, one hand on her hip, the other holding the half-empty tray, chin up, shoulders back. "Jamie."

"This is quite the thing you've got going." Was it the suit he was wearing or his tone that made him seem so out of place? Whatever it was, he was a far cry from the last time she'd seen him, sweaty and shirtless on the boxing ring floor...

Stop it! With a shake of her head, Daisy got the deviant memories under control. "What are you doing here?"

Before he could answer, a couple of massive men elbowed their way to Daisy's side, intent on snatching up what remained on her tray. However, once they were close enough, the shorter man—though he was at least two heads taller than Daisy—punched Jamie on the shoulder. "Hey, man." He tugged on the lapel of his jacket. "A little formal for a party, isn't it?"

"I'm just in between clients."

The bigger guy—taller even than Jamie—pointed to the last piece of strudel on Daisy's tray. "You tried one of these?" His mouth was full as he finished his off. "No kidding, it's the best thing I've ever tasted." He handed Jamie his phone and grabbed the last piece. "Here, take a picture of me eating it in one bite." Jamie fiddled with the guy's phone and snapped a shot of the mammoth man shoving the entire piece of pastry into his mammoth mouth.

"I'll post it to Instagram and Twitter," he informed Daisy after he was done. "I've got like fifty thousand followers or something."

"Yeah," the other guy said. "I'll share it and make sure the other guys on the team share it, too. Maybe it'll go viral."

Daisy's head spun. "That's great. Thanks," she said, though she didn't really know how it would happen.

Seconds later, after the men left to be interviewed by reporters, Daisy leaned toward Jamie and whispered, "If this all goes viral, that would be good for me, right?"

"Yep. Unless it's actually a superbug. Then it's bad."

She quickly got her smile under control. "You know those guys?"

"Sure. They play for the Roughnecks. The big one is Owen Johnson—he's a linebacker. The other one is Eddie Manolo. He's a receiver."

Daisy nodded. A professional football team, right here in her little bakery. It was absolutely crazy, and she had Gloria, her mother and probably Alexander to thank. Taking a deep breath, Daisy caught the scent of Jamie's cologne and was suddenly reminded that she was supposed to be ignoring him. She took one more quick sniff, though, because damn, the man smelled so good.

"What are you doing here?" she repeated the question she'd posed earlier.

"Unfortunately, I'm here on business." He handed her a sealed envelope. "Take a look, please. You need to make a decision before the end of the week." He glanced around. "Depending on how this goes."

"You don't think we can do it, do you? You don't think I can come up with the money."

"I didn't say that. I'm just presenting options, that's all."

Daisy snatched the envelope out of his hand and carried it and the empty tray into the back. She was tempted to drop the envelope into the garbage, but that seemed like asking for trouble, so she ran it upstairs to her apartment and left it on the kitchen counter.

Buying insurance is the best insurance for never needing insurance.

Daisy whipped her head around. "Nana?"

There was no one there. A breeze lifted the gauzy curtain in the open kitchen window, and invisible fingers tickled the back of her neck.

"God, I miss you," she whispered to the ether. "But if you're here, I could really use your help today."

12

THE LAST PLACE Jamie should have been was at the bakery that belonged to his client's soon-to-be ex-wife, though he told himself he was there for professional reasons, to deliver an offer on the building should the fund-raiser not be successful. Though he hoped to hell the fund-raiser was successful.

The truth was he could have waited until after the party to give her the offer. Should have waited until after the party.

He was crossing the line, dammit.

Unfortunately, there was no way Jamie could stay away. He'd tried. But the need to see Daisy outweighed what the costs might be. It was utterly insane, and Jamie wished he knew what was wrong with him so he could get the insanity under control. It wasn't like Daisy wanted to see him—she'd made that plain, though she had laughed at his going viral comment. No, she hadn't laughed. She'd smiled, which was probably more a function of the kind of lighthearted, fun-loving person Daisy Sinclair was than any kind of indicator of how she might or might not feel about him.

And what did it matter, anyway? Nothing could happen

between them. It was over before it'd even started, which was usually the way he liked it.

"Hey." Colin maneuvered through the crowd to join him. After a quick glance at his cohost, Tricia Gordon, he showed Jamie the half-eaten cinnamon bun in his hand and said, "Describe this for me."

Just beyond Colin's outstretched hand stood Daisy, talking again to Owen Johnson and laughing. Her dark curls bounced seductively around her shoulders, reminding him of their little bout in the boxing ring, followed by what happened afterward. Jamie's hands curled into fists as he imagined strands of her hair caught between his fingers. "Perfectly done on the outside, soft and delicious inside. The sweetness tempered by the freshness and goodness of the bread."

"Not bad, little brother."

For a split second, Daisy's gaze shifted from the big linebacker to scan the crowd, and her eyes met Jamie's. She tilted her head to the side as if to ask him a question. With effort, Jamie tore his gaze away. Dropping his voice, he asked, "Any news on what's going on?" He tapped his head. "Up here?"

"More tests next week."

"So it's not a tumor?"

Colin shrugged and before he could answer, Tricia Gordon called, "Colin? We're on in ten."

Nodding at Tricia, he said to Jamie, "We'll talk later."

Jamie rubbed his brow. Things were going to shit and he needed to get the hell out of the bakery before he made it worse. Winding his way through the mob of people, he made his way to the door. But before he could leave, he was stopped by a big man wearing a cowboy hat. It wasn't the hat that caught Jamie's attention, however; it was the guy's familiar, crooked grin. "Dillon. You made it," Jamie said, giving his cousin a slap on the back. He and Colin had spent many summers out on their cousin's ranch in Montana. However, it'd been years since he'd seen Dillon, who was more like a brother than a cousin to him.

"Worked out perfectly with the timing of the National Bull-Riding Championships." Dillon held up a pink frosted cupcake that clashed with his cousin's big, ranch-roughened hands. "This shit is to die for." Frosting first, he shoved the entire cupcake into his mouth, and while his mouth was still full, he said, "I can't get enough."

Out of nowhere, Gloria appeared, nudging Jamie out of the way to address Dillon. "Hey. Why do you think it's okay to move my decor?"

Dillon swiped his hand across the back of his mouth to wipe away the remnants of pink frosting. With his mouth still full of cupcake, he said, "Your *decor* has been blocking the visibility of the hard-working individuals here for the cameras."

Gloria's disgusted shiver was so comical, Jamie decided he had to see the end of this interaction before he left.

"Oh, I'm sorry. Are you the organizer here?" She swept a hand around the room. "Was this your idea?" She poked him in the chest. "Did you bring all these people here?" Poke. "Is Daisy your best friend?" Poke, poke.

"I'm just trying to help." He captured her finger and held on.

She snatched her hand from his. "You can *help* by keeping those big, sloppy hands of yours off my stuff."

Saluting, Dillon said, "As you wish, little lady."

"Oh, my God!" She shook her head at him in exasperation. "Do not call me *little lady*." She stormed off, muttering obscenities beneath her breath.

"Still charming the ladies, I see," Jamie said.

"That one? She's something else." Dillon shook his head. "Are all the women in Chicago that bossy?"

"Yep. Welcome to the big city."

"Thank God I'm just here for the week."

Jamie's phone vibrated in his pocket. It was a text from one of his new clients.

Please call me. It's an emergency.

"I've got to go." He held up the phone. "Work calls. Stop by the club if you've got time."

The front of the bakery was so crowded, Jamie followed a line of people out the side door and, upon exiting, found himself caught in the cross fire of a war, like a snowball fight but with dough instead. He waited for the media to finish taking pictures of hockey players vs. football players throwing balls of dough before making a run for it. Ducking and dodging, he managed to avoid all but one missile as he made his way around the building. He'd had to park his bike four blocks away because it was so busy, and as he walked, he called his client. Right away, he could tell something was wrong.

"Chloe, slow down. Slow down," he said into the phone. "Take a breath and then start from the beginning."

Jamie turned toward the building nearest him and plugged his ear to keep the street noise out so he could focus on his client, who was crying and talking so fast he couldn't make sense of what she was saying. Eventually, the story became clear: her estranged husband had broken into their home and had taken his gun collection, leaving her a note in place of where his guns were stored.

Once Jamie heard what the note said, he interrupted her. "Chloe, listen to me. Hang up the phone right now and call 911. I'll be there in fifteen minutes."

NUMBERS CONTINUED TO be called out all day. Thirty-thousand. One hundred thousand. And it just kept growing and growing. Daisy couldn't believe how much they were raising. This was crazy!

Crazy good.

"Daisy, can you comment on the 'Name the Bakery Item' contest?" Tricia Gordon asked with a huge smile. "So far some of the frontrunners are 'Tempting Twists,'" she said, pointing to the cinnamon twists. "These are 'Devil's Delights'—" she gestured to the chocolate éclairs "—and those lemon bars are now 'Sweet Salvation Bars.'"

Okay, some of what was going on was just *plain* crazy. But when Tricia shoved a microphone in front of her, Daisy smiled. "I love it. I love the names," she lied, hoping she sounded convincing, because the names were a little gimmicky for her taste.

She glanced around. She was not looking for Jamie. Not at all. She needed to escape the cameras, that was it. Catching sight of Gloria rearranging blown-up posters of baked goods on the other side of the room, she said, "If you'll excuse me."

Hurrying over to her friend, she tapped her shoulder and said, "Need some help?"

Gloria growled. She actually bared her teeth and growled. "I'm going to kill him."

"Who?"

Gloria pointed to the same guy she'd argued with early in the day. "The *cowboy.*"

"Does the cowboy have a name?"

"Dillon 'I'm a total jerk' Cross."

"What's he doing?"

"It's not what he's doing—it's what he's *undoing.* Absolutely everything I do, he takes down. Or moves. It's like he's trying to make me mad on purpose. For sport."

"Ignore him." Daisy snagged a fresh tray of goods from a haggard-looking Bruce. She winked at him before he ran back to the kitchen to hide. "Here, have some strudel."

"That's not just strudel anymore. It's 'Strumpet Strudel.'" Gloria waved her off. "And I'm too mad to eat."

"You can't be serious with these names."

"Adopt the names or lose the bakery, babe."

"Okay. Point taken."

Daisy toted the tray outside, where hordes of people were still milling about. Most of the media had gone home by now, and so had a number of the celebrity athletes. The crowd consisted mainly of regular customers, whom she greeted by name, and others who were curious to see what the hubbub was all about. She took a moment to take everything in and check the crowd.

Okay, so maybe she was looking for Jamie, but she certainly wasn't disappointed that he hadn't stuck around for very long. Not at all.

"Why the long face, boss lady?" Lizzie was wearing something that resembled a hazmat suit and had a bowl of dough tucked under her arm.

"Just a little overwhelmed."

Taking her arm, Lizzie said, "I know exactly what you need. Come on." She dragged Daisy through to the side door and pushed her outside to where some sort of war was going on. Lizzie shoved the bowl of dough balls at her. "I get it now," Lizzie said. "Throwing a little dough does make a person feel better."

THE DOUGH STUCK in her hair was going to be a bitch to clean out, but Daisy didn't care. The dough-ball fight in the side yard was the most fun she'd had since—she yanked at a big clump of gluey hair—well, spending time with Jamie at his club had been fun. She braced herself against the vanity in the bathroom, shut her eyes and let her mind wander to that memory. *Fun* didn't quite describe it.

Cleansing?

No.

Sinful?

Nope.

Heavenly?

Maybe.

Her body swayed as excited little palpitations coursed through her veins, like her cells were reliving the experience as she remembered it, boxing that turned into wrestling around on the floor that turned into oral sex. Opening her eyes, she gazed at her reflection in the mirror. No matter what she tried to tell herself, she had it bad for Jamie Forsythe.

"What is wrong with me?" she whispered.

The only explanation for her irrational attraction to the man was a genetic deficiency; she had to have inherited *something* from her mother.

Giving up on getting the dough out of her hair, Daisy went back out to the bakery, which was still busier than ever. Those who remained were paying customers, the kind that had been patronizing the place for years. Daisy went around talking to people, giving and receiving hugs.

"You're not going to lose the bakery, Daisy. We won't let it happen."

"Nana Sin's can't close. We'll do whatever we can to help."

"Your grandmother would be so proud of you."

Eventually, Daisy made her way back to the kitchen to help restock the depleted shelves and to get her emotions under control. Seconds later, Gloria swept into the kitchen like the Energizer Bunny, fresh and as lively as ever.

"How's it going?" Daisy realized she hadn't heard anyone call out an update in hours, partly because she'd been outside slinging dough. She realized she had no idea where she stood, and the unease that had been ever-present leading up to the fund-raiser now blossomed in the pit of her stomach.

"It looks good, Daisy." Gloria grinned and showed her the screen of her phone.

Any unease was blown apart like fireworks because the number on Gloria's screen was ridiculously impossible. "That much?" she whispered.

"Yep."

"Now what happens?"

"At this point it's out of our hands, and we let social media do its thing. Someone tells two friends and they tell two friends and so on."

Making no bones about eavesdropping on their conversation, Lizzie sidled up, peering over Gloria's shoulder at her phone. "Holy shit." She wrapped her flour-covered arms around Daisy's waist and squeezed. "You're going to do it, boss. Can't you feel it?" Letting her go, Lizzie turned and called to the staff, "We're going to do it, people. We're going to save Nana Sin's!"

13

"WE'RE NOT GOING to do it, are we?" Daisy stared at the computer screen. She and Gloria sat at her kitchen table, watching the numbers. They hadn't moved since 6:30 p.m. that evening. It was ten thirty now. She had an hour and a half to come up with the rest of the money. It wasn't going to happen.

"Four hundred thirty thousand is a lot of money." Gloria forced a smile, but Daisy saw the disappointment in her friend's face. "We raised a shitload, Daise. Maybe Alan will accept it if you promise to pay the rest over the next six months." She twisted her lips, knowing it wasn't going to work.

Despite everything Gloria had done, they had failed, and Daisy had no one to blame but herself.

"By then your mom might be able to help and…"

Daisy shook her head and slid a large legal-sized envelope in front of Gloria. It was the envelope that Jamie had dropped off during the party.

"What's this?"

"An offer. Jamie gave it to me yesterday." Even now, even after everything, saying Jamie's name made something unexpected happen in her abdomen.

Before opening the envelope, Gloria took a deep drink of wine, as if that would fortify her for whatever the envelope contained. She pulled out the documents and read them through.

"So, Alan found a buyer, huh?"

"Yep."

She flipped back to the front page. "A French bistro?" Gloria looked through the documents again. "I don't see anything about the Nana Sin name—do you get to keep it?"

Daisy shrugged. "That was supposed to be the deal."

"Well, that's something, isn't it?"

With a halfhearted shrug, Daisy gazed around the kitchen of the only real home she'd ever known. It wasn't just the name of the bakery that mattered to her. It was this place. Every nook and cranny. Every wall and window. Every part of it was a part of her grandmother. A part of her.

How the hell was she supposed to let it go?

"I'm so sorry."

Daisy met her friend's gaze, touched by the tears sliding down her cheeks. "I will never forget what you did for me, Glo. You are the absolute best friend, and I don't know how I can ever repay you."

"You would do the same for me. I know you would." She raised her glass to Daisy. "And I know that you will move past this and succeed. One day."

Daisy touched her glass to Gloria's. "Maybe. One day. But that day is not today."

STRANGE, DAISY FELT absolutely nothing—as if she was in one of those deprivation chambers and all sensory stimuli had been removed. Sounds were muted: the ring of telephones, the sound of her heels on the tile, the opening and closing of doors. All the typical office din blended into crackling white noise in her head.

She knocked on the meeting room door and when Jamie opened it, even her stomach had no response to him. Not to his size, his towering height, or his pleasing, masculine scent.

"Come in, Daisy."

In her current state of mind, ordinary things struck Daisy as odd. For example, someone telling her to come in. She'd knocked, hadn't she? What was she supposed to do if not come in? What were her options? To be obstinate and stand outside? Throw a temper tantrum? Lie on her desk and throw dough at the ceiling?

The ceiling. Hmm. She wondered if she should bother to have that cleaned before the sale went through.

Nah.

"Have a seat."

She sat. That was when she noticed that Alan wasn't there, and in his place was a dark-haired woman already sitting at the table. "Who are you?"

"This is Priya Naidoo," Jamie said.

"Hi, Daisy." The woman stood and shook Daisy's hand.

"Priya's your lawyer. Now, you have the right to retain alternate council if you don't want Priya, but, as was explained to you at our last meeting, you are required to have independent legal advice."

"Got it."

"So, would you like to retain Ms. Naidoo's services?"

"Yep." She held out her hand. "Give me the papers. I'll sign whatever needs to be signed."

Priya cast a glance at Jamie before moving next to Daisy, sliding a file folder along the table top.

"I'll leave you two to it, then," Jamie said.

Daisy suddenly felt something, she wasn't sure what, when Jamie left the room. Anger? Annoyance? Despair?

"I've looked over your file and—"

Daisy put her hand on the papers and pulled them close. "I don't care what it says. Please. Just tell me where to sign."

"I know this is hard, but it's my obligation to make sure you understand everything you are signing. For example—" Priya flipped through some pages "—here are the terms of the sale. You need to vacate the property in a month."

An invisible fist punched Daisy square in the gut. She leaned over, the wind sucked right out of her. The lawyer stopped speaking and waited. Finally, Daisy felt a soft, feminine touch on her back.

"I've been through it myself, Ms. Sinclair. I know how hard it is."

Daisy raised her face, wanting to challenge the other woman, but found only kindness and compassion in her expression.

"I know you won't believe this, but the one thing I've learned in this business is that, while starting over is scary and never, ever easy, it's often the very thing we need most."

Now the woman sounded like her mother, except that for some strange reason, the words were more palatable coming from her mouth. "Okay," she said with a small nod. "Let's go through the paperwork."

In less time than Daisy imagined it would take to split up and reconfigure every aspect of her life, everything was signed. Once the papers went in front of a judge, Daisy would be divorced.

And without a livelihood.

And alone.

And…tired. So tired.

Daisy walked through a thick, murky fog as she exited the building. She was vaguely aware of Jamie's presence and of him asking her if she was okay. But it honestly took too much energy to respond. Even the parts of her that so often responded to Jamie—against her wishes—were subdued.

Outside the building, she sat on a bench.

Now what?

Her phone rang and Daisy made a grab for it. She didn't know why, really. Maybe because it gave her something to do.

"Daisy, it's me."

"Mom?"

"How are you, honey?"

Honey? Daisy couldn't remember the last time her mother had called her honey.

"How do you think I am?"

There was a pause and then Cynthia said quietly, "I'm sorry."

"How'd you know?"

"Gloria told me. She said you were signing the papers this morning."

"Yep."

"Do you want to come over?"

"No."

More silence.

"Okay, then, Mom. I'll talk to you—"

"Listen," her mother interrupted her before she could hang up. "Do you remember my friend Julie?"

Daisy had to think for a second. "Yeah, sure. Why?"

"Well, she's having a sort of garden party."

"That's nice." Why the hell was her mother telling her about her friend right now? As if Daisy cared about her mother's friend's garden party.

"She asked me to invite you, as well."

"Me? Why?"

"Well…"

Daisy sighed. "Mom, I'm really not in the mood for a social gathering." What was her mother thinking? Oh. Right. She wasn't thinking. As usual.

"But it's not until next Friday and—" Cynthia stopped. In a soft voice, she continued, "Never mind. Of course you're not in the mood. The last thing you want to do is celebrate."

She got that right.

"Forget I mentioned it."

"Okay."

"I'll talk to you soon—"

Wait a second... "Celebrate?" Daisy interrupted. "What's the occasion?"

Her mother laughed. It was a happy yet somewhat awkward sound. "Well," she said, and then cleared her throat. "Alexander asked me to marry him. It's an engagement party."

DAISY SINCLAIR WALKED right past him as if she didn't even know him. Or rather, as if she knew him only as her ex-husband's lawyer, not as the man who'd most recently made love to her. He retreated into his office, staring out the window, watching her collapse on the bench outside the building, the very picture of dejection.

He forced himself to watch and to feel the pressure build in his chest. Once again, he'd failed a woman he cared about, which was exactly why he'd stayed away from attachment in the first place. It inevitably came crashing down, leaving nothing but hurt. He leaned his shoulder against the window frame. Why did he care about Daisy so much, anyway? Why had he put his job on the line for her? They'd spent one wonderful night together, but that was it. Of course, there was the incident in the gym. That was... Jamie didn't have words for what that was. Incredibly hot?

He groaned.

The reality was, he might not have known Daisy very long, but he knew what kind of woman she was: the kind you came home to every night and had a long-term relationship with. She was the kind of woman who was searching for happily-ever-after. Even after divorce, she probably still believed in it. That was not something Jamie could provide, nor what he believed.

He was a cynic. He didn't believe in happily-ever-after. He believed in fun for now because happiness never lasted.

He finally turned from the window, finding some solace in the fact that Daisy was now speaking to someone on the phone—no surprise, since the woman had a wide network of friends—and made his way to his desk, where his inbox overflowed.

Helen buzzed him on his intercom. "Alan Smith is ready to sign when you are."

Rubbing his temples, Jamie leaned his elbows on his desk.

Fuck.

His fingers curled into tight fists. There was no way he could face Daisy's ex right now because he might do something unspeakable, like punch the guy in the face. The fact that the thought gave him a warped sense of pleasure was confirmation he needed to pass this off.

"Lyle's around. Get him to finish up with the paperwork. I've got something else pressing at the moment."

It was true, sort of. He pulled the file for Chloe Van Der Kamp. He'd met with her yesterday after her husband had broken into the house and stolen the gun collection. It turned out there was a history of violence there. They'd spent the better part of the morning drawing up an affidavit.

Jamie checked his watch. He had to be in court in an hour to petition for a protective order for Mrs. Van Der Kamp. But instead of gathering everything together and getting ready to go, Jamie sat at his desk and rested his head in his hands, images of his sister surfacing behind closed lids. This always happened whenever he had to do this. The worst part was, no matter how hard he tried, he could not see his sister as she'd been, gentle and sweet, full of life and potential, but only as they'd found her, lifeless and beaten.

DAISY HAD NO intention of going to an engagement party. No way. Though her mother had offered to have the party postponed, Daisy had insisted that Cynthia not change the date for her benefit. That would just have made her feel worse. But it didn't mean she had to attend the stupid thing. Daisy had plans and they involved staying home and moping. There was nothing wrong with a good mope when your life had completely disintegrated. She hadn't showered since yesterday, when they'd closed the doors to Nana Sin's for good. Now she wore her grungiest clothes, had her hair tied up in an unappealing knot at the top of her head, and was ready to clean cupboards. It was best to have something to do while moping. Made the moping less mopey.

Standing on a chair, she started with the neglected cupboard above the refrigerator. Daisy hadn't opened it in years, and she was surprised by the contents: old tins, chipped plates and random, cracked cups and saucers.

"Honestly, Nana. What were you holding on to these things for?" Daisy muttered as she hopped down off the chair. She picked up a plate and turned it over. It wasn't even good china, just regular, daily crockery. She momentarily considered tossing the plates at a wall—Greek-style—but decided against it. Her days of throwing things at walls and ceilings were over. Now it was time to clean.

She found a trash bag under the sink and swept the broken crockery into the bag. The tins were a different story. Some were antique and others were holiday containers her grandmother used to fill with treats to give to friends. Maybe she'd hold on to those.

From the boxes lining the floor, Daisy selected a big one and began opening up the tins to stack them. Among them was a small tea tin, and when Daisy picked it up, she heard the *tink* of something rattling around inside.

The skin on the back of her neck pricked as though someone was behind her, softly blowing. The prickling sensation crept up to the top of her scalp as she removed the lid and peered inside.

Her grandmother's diamond engagement ring winked back at her. Carefully Daisy removed it and held it up to the light.

"What are you doing in there?" Daisy whispered. She and her mother had looked all over for the ring after Nana died. They'd thought it had been lost.

As if in answer to Daisy's question, the bells of her grandmother's clock on the mantel rang, letting her know it was six o'clock. The engagement party would be starting in an hour. If she hurried, she'd just be able to make it.

HER MOTHER'S FRIEND Julie lived in the exclusive Lincoln Park district, and Daisy stood in a quiet corner of the beautiful garden, an untouched flute of champagne in her hand, wearing a brightly flowered dress that did not reflect her mood. She'd have worn black—she was definitely in more of a black mood than a big splashy flower mood—but as Daisy went through her closet, she realized she actually didn't own a black dress.

Huh.

From where she stood, she watched her mother laughing and smiling. She marveled at the fact that she'd never seen her so lively. It was weird how she could be there, observing her mother, who appeared happier than Daisy had ever seen her before in her life, while Daisy, on the other hand, had never felt more heavy-hearted. Was that the universe's warped sense of humor or was it some karmic balance?

"I'm so glad you made it, Daisy."

"Hey, Alex." Daisy shook herself out of her metaphysical musing and tried to smile at her soon-to-be stepfather. Unfortunately, her lips weren't exactly cooperating.

"You look—"

"Terrible," Daisy supplied. "We're family now. You don't need to lie." She knew her eyes were swollen and her cheeks splotchy.

"I was going to say sad." His brows drew together. "I'm really sorry you're going through such a hard time right now."

Daisy nodded. "Me, too."

"If there's anything I can do, let me know."

Using the flute to point at her mother on the other side of the garden, Daisy said, "Just keep on making my mom happy. That's more than enough." She set the glass down to open her bag. "And there's something I found today that I wanted to give you."

She had placed the ring in a proper ring box, and now she removed it from her purse and showed it to Alex. "I'm sure you've already got a fabulous ring picked out, and I doubt if my mom would even want this, but it belonged to her mother and I remember…" Her words trailed off as a tightness seized her throat. She had a memory of her mother asking Nana if she could wear it because her grandmother rarely did. That was a long time ago.

"We haven't chosen rings yet." He accepted the box. "This is beautiful. Thanks." He took a step closer and gave her a big hug. "And thanks for coming. Your mom didn't expect you to show up. I'm really glad you did."

The man had the good grace to leave before her tears

began to fall unchecked down her cheeks. Daisy thought she'd cried herself out earlier in the week. First the signing of the papers, then when she'd had to give everyone at work their notices. That was a bad day. Bruce had had a breakdown in the kitchen, and there were more than a few tears shed by the rest of the staff.

Watching them all leave on the last day shattered Daisy's already broken heart.

"It's not your fault," Lizzie had said, patting her shoulder while Daisy fought tears.

"It is my fault," Daisy had said. "I should have figured something out sooner. I left it too long."

"Everyone will get back on their feet. Don't worry."

Wiping her nose, Daisy recalled asking, "What about you, Lizzie? What will you do?"

In typical Lizzie fashion, she'd shrugged. "I don't know. I'll find something. You know, there's a whole big world out there. So many opportunities. So many possibilities. It's kind of exciting and terrifying all at once."

"Please don't say one door closes and three more open or I might lose it."

Crinkling her nose, Lizzie said, "I've seen you lose it, boss lady. It's not pretty. Not a big fan of seeing that whole thing—" Lizzie made a circular gesture in Daisy's general direction "—again. Nope. No, thank you."

Daisy had given her a fierce hug, saying, "You've been the best employee I've ever had."

"You've been the most entertaining boss. By far." Lizzie hugged back just as fiercely. "Now, go see what's behind one of those other doors."

As Daisy recalled the conversation, she found herself smiling. God, she was going to miss Lizzie and her quirky ways. However, the minute she realized who was approaching from the other side of the garden, her smile fell right off, onto the grass.

The problem was, while Jamie Forsythe was the cause of so much distress in her life, he still had an immediate effect on her body. Some unknown muscle at the base of her tummy fluttered, her lungs forgot—temporarily—how to draw oxygen and her broken heart beat out of sync, as if there really were two parts vying for control.

Jamie stopped in front of her, looking cool and casual in his cotton shirt and trousers. His hair was swept back, mussed, as though he'd just run his fingers through it. Daisy's fingers twitched involuntarily with the memory of doing the very same thing.

The sight of him had Daisy playing the "if only" game. If only things had been different. If only they had met at a different stage of life. If only he hadn't been hired by her ex. If only he didn't drive a motorcycle. If only he really was his brother, the food critic…

"If onlys" are a waste of energy. What-ifs are so much more productive.

"I know," Daisy whispered. "But give me tonight to 'if only.' I promise, I'll 'what if' tomorrow."

14

HE'D JUST BEEN thinking about Daisy and then, there she was, standing all alone in the corner of the yard, as if Jamie had somehow conjured her. He hadn't seen her since she'd signed the papers in his office. He'd been tempted to call her so many times, to see how she was. To ask if she was okay. But he'd controlled the urge.

It was for the best. In much too short a time, he'd become much too close to Daisy Sinclair, to the point that his thoughts about her were completely disproportionate to the short amount of time he'd spent with her. Just when he thought he was getting a handle on the situation and figured he'd never see her again, she was standing in front of him. Her cheeks ablaze, her eyes bright—beautiful— muttering something beneath her breath. A curse word?

He wouldn't blame her.

"Are you stalking me?" she asked, hands on her hips.

"Stalking? No. A.J. invited me."

Daisy shook her head, her hair brushing the skin of her shoulders. He couldn't decide which was more distracting, the swish of her soft hair against her skin or the sight of her bare shoulders.

"Who the hell is A.J.?"

Jamie gave her a perplexed look. "A.J. The groom."

"Alexander? You know Alexander?"

Jamie nodded. "Yes. He's a member of my club."

"He boxes? No way."

"Yes, he does. How do you know him?"

"Ah, he's marrying my mother."

Jamie blinked in disbelief. Cynthia was Daisy's mother?

"I know, right?" Daisy said with a sardonic smile. "It's okay. I get it all the time. Cynthia and I are nothing alike."

"I wouldn't say that," Jamie said, tilting his head to observe her anew. Both women were natural beauties. But where Cynthia was serious, Daisy had a certain zest. Where Daisy was soft and sweet and deliciously curvy, Cynthia was all sharp angles and hard planes. He was willing to bet Daisy smiled more, laughed more, enjoyed life more. Or at least, she had before she'd met him.

"Small world," he muttered when he realized he'd been studying Daisy for longer than was polite. Not that being polite really mattered between them anymore.

They stood in silence for a few seconds. Daisy's pretty face went through a whole range of expressions, smiling one second, then looking vexed and scowling the next.

"So," she said. "How's the divorce business?"

"Daisy…"

She warded him off with raised hands. "It's okay. I'm totally over it."

"No, you're not."

She met his gaze. "No. I'm not."

Jamie took a drink of his beer. "I don't know if you care but… I've been thinking about you, and I just want you to know, I'm really sorry."

"It's funny," she said. "People keep saying that, yet it really doesn't change anything." She nibbled on her lower lip, and he wondered if it was an attempt to hide the quiver in her chin. If so, it wasn't working.

Yes. That was the other difference between Daisy and Cynthia. On the few occasions he'd met Cynthia, he'd considered her to be standoffish. Daisy, on the other hand, showed every single emotion she felt. Right now, he could see how upset she was.

"I don't know what else to say, Daisy," he told her quietly.

With her arms crossed over her chest, Daisy responded, "Maybe that's because there's nothing left for either of us to say to one another."

Her words were like an unexpected jab to the solar plexus. "So that's it?"

"Yes, Jamie. It is."

Wow. Jamie rubbed the indentation between his brows, the one that had become much deeper in the last few weeks. He agreed with Daisy—logically—that things were over, had been for a while, and should definitely stay that way. Yet now that she'd articulated his very thoughts, he wanted nothing more than to rally against them and prove to her that they were both wrong. He longed to step closer, breathe in the scent of her skin—what flavor would she be today? Vanilla? Cinnamon? Or something more subtle, like rosemary?

His fingers yearned to caress the place where her hair brushed her bare shoulders. He longed to watch her lids grow heavy as he drew a line down her spine, not stopping when he reached the top of her lovely ass, but cupping her through her dress and squeezing, pulling her up against him so that she could feel the effect she had on him.

But no matter what he wanted physically, the sadness and accusation in her gaze spoke to his logic center, and it won out. "I get it, Daisy. Loud and clear. You don't want to see me again. I understand." He tipped his beer to her before drinking, and the fizz burned his throat as he swallowed.

At that point, he should have left to join the other guests—after all, he knew a number of people at this party—but for some reason he was reluctant to leave her side, perhaps recognizing that the minute he did, he would never see Daisy again.

In the end, Daisy took the choice away from him. "Goodbye, Jamie." Her lower lip trembled. With her head held high, she turned away, leaving him standing in the corner of a garden, drinking his beer as he watched the most beautiful, interesting, exciting woman he'd ever met walk away.

And he did it without a fight.

DAISY HAD BARELY taken ten steps before her mother spotted her and rushed across the patio in her direction. Daisy had never witnessed her mother "rushing" before in her life. It was a confusing sight.

"Daisy!" She held her ring finger up, displaying Nana's ring. "I love it. I love it so much!" Cynthia wrapped her thin arms around her and squeezed.

God, for someone so skinny, her mother was really strong.

"How did you know?" She pulled away, her face beaming as she continued to talk without giving Daisy a chance to answer. "I thought it was lost. Thought I'd never see it again. But here it is." She held her hand out again and the diamonds sparkled in the waning sunlight. "Did you know I've always loved this ring? Alex and I haven't been able to find one that I like, and now I realize it's because I always imagined myself wearing *this* one."

Had Daisy inadvertently entered the Twilight Zone? She'd never heard her mother "babble" either, which was exactly what her mother was doing. The world had gone completely bonkers.

Patting her mother on the back, she said, "I'm glad you like it." When she started to pull away, her mother held on with all that weird, skinny strength of hers.

"I'm so glad you're here. I didn't think you'd make it and when I saw you, I meant to come over right away to thank you for coming and then Alexander gave me the ring and then everyone wanted to see and—"

"Uh, Mom? I have to go now."

Cynthia finally let up, moving to grasp Daisy's hands. She smiled with a weird mixture of happiness, giddiness, and googly-eyed loopiness.

"It's been a long week," Daisy explained, expecting her mother to insist she stay.

But she didn't. Nodding sympathetically, Cynthia said, "I understand. I'll walk you out. There's something I need to ask you before you go." With her arm linked through Daisy's, Cynthia guided her through the house, introducing her to people as they went.

"This is my daughter—isn't she lovely?"

"This is Daisy. Yes, the one and only."

By the time they got to the front door, they'd had fifteen miniconversations, and Daisy was surprised at how much her mother's friends seemed to know about her. Once out on the street, Daisy unlinked her arm and said, "What did you want to ask me?"

Licking her lips, Cynthia smiled a hopeful, wobbly, uncertain smile. "I'd like you to stand up for me at the wedding."

"Me?" Daisy held a hand to her chest. "Why me?"

"Well, you are my daughter."

"But," Daisy said, confused, "we're not even close." Motioning to the house, she added, "What about Julie? Or one of your other friends? You have a ton you could ask."

"Wow." Cynthia stood up straighter as she blinked back at Daisy. "I really have been a terrible mother, haven't I?"

"No," Daisy said, automatically. Then she stopped herself. She was way too tired to play whatever game this was. "Actually." She chewed her lip. "You were pretty terrible."

A burst of air exploded between Cynthia's pursed lips and Daisy prepared herself for the excuses. *I was only seventeen when I had you. I never planned to get pregnant. Your father left the moment he found out.* Blah, blah, blah.

"You're right."

Daisy flinched. "What did you say?"

"I said you're right. I've been horrible and I—" Just when Daisy didn't think her mother could surprise her more, a big fat tear escaped out of the corner of her eye and crept down her cheek, leaving a glistening streak through her makeup.

Cynthia was crying? Daisy couldn't remember seeing her mother cry, and the result was a huge lump lodged low in her throat.

"When Alexander came into my life, well, things changed for me, and I realized something important."

"What?" Daisy asked slowly, because the thing stuck in her throat—the big, hot, messy thing—made it difficult to speak.

"I've been sabotaging myself my whole life." She tapped her chest. "Me. I was the one who made the mistakes. I was the one who..." She paused to turn away, but not before Daisy saw two more tears streak down her cheeks. After a deep breath, she continued, "I was the one who messed up I was the one to blame. Not you. It was never your fault She turned back and placed her hand on Daisy's chee "But I made you feel like it was, didn't I?"

When Daisy didn't answer, her mother nodded. "I am so sorry," she whispered.

That did it. The thing in her windpipe broke open, scalding her throat, scorching her numb heart and stinging her eyes. Daisy couldn't reply because the thing had taken over her voice, her chest, her face…her whole body.

"I hope you will give me another chance." Her mother's face looked so young and hopeful and human that it broke Daisy's heart.

"Of course." Daisy hiccuped. "Of course I'll give you another chance. If you'll give me another chance." Her mother's gasping breath made it hard to continue, but Daisy did anyway. She had to. "And…of course I'll stand up for you at your wedding. I'd be honored."

"You will?" Those strong, skinny arms wrapped so tightly around her, Daisy could barely breathe.

But strangely, Daisy liked it, and she hugged her mother right back. Maybe the changes she'd noticed were real. And if so, didn't changing the dynamics of a relationship take effort from both parties? "Mom?"

"Yes?"

Her mother let up on her vise grip, allowing Daisy to take a deep breath. "Thanks for all the help with the fund-raiser."

"You're welcome. I just wish we could have done more."

Daisy pulled away. "More? You and Alex single-handedly brought in all of those celebrities. That was incredible."

Her mother pulled a face. "No, we didn't."

"Yes, you did."

"No." Cynthia laughed through her tears. "That was all Jamie."

"Jamie?"

"Yep."

"But…how?"

"Lots of those guys belong to his club."

"Why would he do that?"

"Why do you think?"

"But he—"

"Was doing his job. While trying to protect you." Her mother found a packet of tissues in her handbag and passed one to Daisy. "The man is smitten with you, Daisy. And I might not be the best person to give advice, but I can tell you this. He's one of the good guys. Do not let him go without a fight."

TODAY WAS THE day the movers were coming to pack up the bakery. Daisy had spent the week organizing everything, donating all the foodstuffs to the local food bank, itemizing what would be staying and what she'd be putting in storage. How long things would stay in storage kind of depended on Daisy's cash flow. After the sale went through, she would be able to pay off the mortgage she'd had to take out, and the line of credit for the new stoves. That left barely enough for a down payment on a house. Of course there was the fund-raiser money but that was earmarked for some future business endeavor and Daisy didn't have the energy to figure out what that might be yet, which was why she wasn't willing to sell her practically new industrial ovens. "You can stay with me until you get back on your feet," Gloria had told her, which was a really sweet offer, but Daisy felt the best thing for her would be to find something of her own to rent for now—somewhere she could settle, if only temporarily, but that would give her a sense of home and familiarity.

"If that's what you want to do, then let me help you. I'v got some contacts. I'll line up some places, and we can apartment hunting together. It'll be fun!"

So, today, instead of being there for the big move, D

had enlisted Lizzie's help to oversee everything in the bakery so that she could go apartment hunting with Gloria.

Seriously. Gloria was the best friend. Ever.

Daisy waved to her out the window when she pulled up in front of the bakery and was halfway down the stairs when she realized she'd left her phone beside her bed. Hurrying back up the stairs, she located the phone, unplugged it from the charger and turned to leave.

"Ouch!"

Hopping on one foot, she held on to the other, trying to figure out what she'd stepped on. Something shiny and round was on the floor beside the bed. Stooping down, Daisy picked up the culprit.

A cuff link?

Weird. It had been over a month since Jamie had been to her place. How could she not have noticed his cuff link on the floor before now? Turning it over in her hand, she was overcome by a vivid memory of Jamie there, in her bedroom, on her bed, tossing the cuff links onto the bedside table so he could remove his shirt. The image of his chest was so vivid, the muscles, the tattoos…the bruises.

I own a club. A fight club.

All of those professional athletes came to help out because of Jamie. Why had he done that?

He's one of the good guys.

Was he? Daisy thought about all the things that had happened between them, ticking them off on her fingers as she recounted them. One, he'd lied about who he was… but then he said he'd done it to protect his brother. Two, he'd seduced her, but that wasn't true, either. She was the one who couldn't keep her hands off him—he'd even given her the choice to invite him up to her place or not. Three, he'd worked for Alan but then…that was only because he'd taken over for Alan's lawyer without knowing who Alan was. Four, he'd lied about knowing her, but that was so he could help her.

He had jeopardized his career to help her?

Huh.

Five, the gym. He'd let her punch him. Hard. And then...

The honk from Gloria's horn curbed that memory before it had a chance to start. Two more honks followed by one long one and she locked the door, ran down the stairs and hopped into Gloria's car, Jamie's cuff link tucked into her pocket for safekeeping.

BY SIX O'CLOCK that evening, Daisy had found herself a new place. It was a supercute loft in Lincoln Park, available immediately, with high ceilings, a huge kitchen and a lovely, sunny bedroom with a dormer window seat that Daisy absolutely loved. Gloria had had to leave her partway through the day to go stage a house, which was fine with Daisy. She had a mission. She'd accomplished item one on her list: find a place to live. Now it was time for item two.

All day long the cuff link in her pocket had been a constant reminder of what she needed to do. Now she stood on the sidewalk outside the old warehouse where Jamie's boxing club was located, staring up at the building.

"Hey, Daisy," a male voice called from a few feet away. "What are you doing here?"

She turned to see Alex walking her way. "I was looking for Jamie."

"I'm sure he's inside. He's here pretty much every night."

Daisy followed Alex up the steps to the big double doors, which were locked, but he had a key. He opened the door and held it so Daisy could go in first. The familiar smell of the place was like a slap in the face, and she plugged her nose.

"What?" Alex laughed. "You think this is bad? You

should try a hockey locker room. The smell's ten times worse."

"You played hockey?"

"Fifteen years. I played for Chicago when they won the NorrisCup in 2007." He showed Daisy the big, gaudy, be-jeweled ring on his hand.

"Wow." She touched it, marveling at how much she didn't know about her soon-to-be stepfather. "That's cool."

The thing she liked about her mother's boyfriend was that he didn't make a big deal about his accomplishments and just glanced around the gym, nodding at a group of guys standing nearby who all called him A.J.

What a change from the last time she'd been there. Alone. With Jamie.

"It's really busy here." Daisy recognized some men from the fund-raiser, including Owen and Eddie, working out with the big bags in the corner.

"Yeah, this place has a good vibe." Alex laughed as Daisy waved her hand in front of her nose. "I said *vibe*, not smell." He acknowledged a guy walking by with an upward nod, "Plus," he said in a low voice, "we all like taking a turn in the ring every now and then. It's a good way to blow off steam." He winked. "Don't tell your mother."

"I won't." Daisy winked back.

"If you're looking for Jamie, he's right there." Bending so that he was on her level, he pointed to the men in the ring.

Daisy's stomach did a triple back flip culminating in a belly flop at the sight of him.

Sweating.

Shirtless.

Blood dripping from a cut beside his eye.

Dodging the fists of a man as tall as he was with probably at least twenty to thirty pounds on him.

"Oh, my," Daisy whispered.

Alex chuckled. "Jamie loves a good fight. He's a tough son of a bitch, for a lawyer." He grinned and gave Daisy a one-armed hug. "Later."

Daisy watched him go, deciding once and for all that she really, really liked the man who was about to become her stepfather. God, that was a weird thought. She'd never had a father before, and Alex seemed more like an older brother than a dad.

Whatever. As long as her mom was happy, she was happy. Daisy turned back to the ring and, like a needle drawn to magnetic north, was propelled forward. A couple of empty chairs sat ringside and she took one, dragging it closer and sitting down to watch. The two men circled each other slowly, looking as if they'd been at it a while. Sweat bathed their skin, and Daisy noticed Jamie wasn't the only one who was bleeding—the other guy was, too.

Hey, wait a second…was that the cowboy from the fund-raiser?

Yes, it was.

She shook her head, realizing just how much Jamie had worked behind the scenes to help her. She continued to watch the fight, marveling at the notion that men could be friends one second—hadn't she seen Jamie clapping the cowboy on the back at the fund-raiser?—and willingly fighting the next. Yet she had to admit, there was something morbidly fascinating about watching two big, strong men hit each other. When Jamie took a hard right cross to the jaw, Daisy covered her mouth to keep from gasping out loud. When he retaliated with a combo, Daisy articulated her enthusiasm with a "Yes!"

She squeezed her knees together and leaned forward, hands pressed together before her face.

Beating the shit out of someone can be very cathartic.

She knew the truth of that statement firsthand, but

watching Jamie go at it? The intensity of his expression, the play of his muscles across his back, his shoulders and abdomen, the force behind his punches, the expulsion of oxygen upon absorption of a blow? Yes. She could see this was more than just physical exercise. He was exorcising demons.

What sort of demons did Jamie Forsythe have, Daisy wondered.

Then she forgot to wonder because she suddenly saw herself up there in the ring, pummeling him with all she had, the crazy energy that coursed through her as she gave in to the physicality of it. The way Jamie let her do it…

The way she needed more.

Even now, her heart was beating erratically, as if she was the one fighting, not watching. Her palms were damp, her tummy trembled…low, low, low. At one point she had to shut her eyes because watching became too overwhelming, but behind her shuttered lids was a replay of what happened after she fought Jamie.

Drawing his thumb into her mouth, his hands in her shorts, him wrenching her legs wide and devouring her.

How much she loved it.

How hard she came.

When she finally opened her eyes, the fight was over. The two men stood center ring and clumsily patted each other on the back with their big gloves. "Thanks, coz. Brings back memories, don't it?"

"Yep," Jamie said. "Memories of kicking your ass too many times to count."

"Right," the cowboy drawled. "In your dreams." Using a towel draped over the rope right in front of Daisy, the cowboy wiped sweat off his face and then noticed her standing there. "Heya, Daisy." He turned to Jamie. "Jimbo, your girlfriend's here." He turned back to Daisy and grinned.

A sweet heat enveloped Daisy at the word *girlfriend*. She hadn't been someone's girlfriend in a very long time, and while Jamie wasn't her boyfriend, she couldn't stop her body's favorable response to the term.

However, her shy smile froze when she met Jamie's dark, smoldering gaze.

"Hi," she said, feeling fluttery and uncertain. "Good fight."

Jamie didn't smile back. Neither did he say anything. He simply grabbed his towel and water bottle, ducked through the ropes on the other side of the ring and, without a backward glance, stalked away.

15

His cousin Dillon was an ass and Daisy Sinclair was not his girlfriend. They'd barely even dated. The fact that he still couldn't stop thinking about her? Still had the urge to pick up the phone and call her, drop by her place and ring her doorbell? Tell her how badly he needed to see her? That was all probably the result of misplaced frustration, and he had it under control. He was managing the way he always managed, by coming to the gym every day, sparring with whomever he found there, using the ring as an outlet for the restless, unsettled beast that had made a home in his gut.

That beast was what had prompted him to start the club with Colin six years ago, after Sarah had died. One too many bar fights in the years after her death, and he'd almost gotten himself disbarred.

Since then, the ring was the only place Jamie could go to forget, taking out his frustration and angst over Sarah, over clients, over personal issues—Daisy Sinclair, for example— it didn't matter. The only thing that seemed to settle the beast was lacing up the gloves.

Except for lately.

Lately, it was as though the beast was unquenchable and no matter how many sparring partners Jamie found, how many times he whupped someone's ass or had his own ass whupped, the restless feeling never let up. He thought today might be different; he and his cousin had been fighting since they were kids and it was always a good match. Then Daisy showed up and the beast bellowed.

Why the hell did she have that effect on him?

Up until he'd met her, life had been perfect. He had a good job, one he enjoyed…for the most part. It paid well. He had a healthy sex life with women who weren't interested in long-term relationships—though, to be honest, he couldn't remember the last woman's name. Jess? Ashley?

Whatever. He was happy.

He'd been happy until Daisy Sinclair came into his life with her curvy, sensual body, her lust for life and her ability to satisfy his appetite in pretty much all the important areas of life: food, sex, passion, conversation. But if there was one thing he knew for a fact, it was that that shit didn't last and she'd done him a favor by telling him it was over. She was damn definitive about it, too, exactly what he needed.

So, why the hell was she here?

After showering, he strode out of the locker room, hoping she'd left, except the thought of her being gone prodded the restless thing in his gut, making it poke at his ribs and elbow his heart.

Of course she was still there, only now she was standing by the full-size bags, surrounded by a group of men. Big men. The sight left him feral and illogical.

Pushing his way into the circle, he wrapped his hand firmly around Daisy's upper arm and said in a low voice, "A word, if you don't mind."

She glanced up at him and blushed.

Dammit. The woman was deadly. A cross between blushing school girl and sultry vixen. His own warring personalities, protector and asshole, vied for control when she looked at him like that. Well, no more. She'd met the gentler, softer Jamie. Time for her to meet the other one, the real him.

He yanked her across the floor to his office at the back of the gym, opened the door and pushed her inside.

"Jamie, there's no need to be—"

He didn't give her a chance to finish. Backing her right up against the wall, he said, "What are you doing here?"

"*You* brought me here."

"That was different." He leaned down. She smelled sweet, like vanilla, an innocent scent that drove him batshit crazy, making him to do stupid, stupid things. "You need to leave." He pressed his body against hers.

"Okay. I will, but…"

"You can't just come in here, Daisy. This is a private club. Private." He increased the tension on her wrists and raised her arms above her head.

"Right. I understand. It's just…"

"This is a place where guys can be guys. Without worrying about women." He leaned closer, rubbing his cheek against her soft curls.

"Of course. Makes sense." Daisy's heavy breathing bathed his face in peppermint.

He inhaled deeply. Peppermint and vanilla. Jesus. He placed his face right next to her ear. "Why are you here?" he whispered.

"Ah," she panted. "You forgot something at my place." She paused to take another breath. "I just came to drop it off."

"Is that right?" He dropped lower, nuzzling into that crease between her jaw and shoulder, breathing in deeply. Barely controlling the urge to devour her.

"It's in my pocket." She moved her hips against him, against the thigh he'd wedged between her legs, and the result of her not-so-innocent gyration was a searing heat aimed right at his groin. "Don't move," he growled.

"O-kay."

Jamie pulled back long enough to observe her expression. Her pretty eyes were wide with…something. Fear? Lust? Passion? A combination of all three? He groaned because he had no clue what he was doing anymore. His body's reaction to her was total instinct: needing to be close, needing to grind—body to body—totally ignoring that small part of his brain telling him to back far away from Daisy Sinclair.

"It's in my pocket." She said again and twisted her pelvis, presenting her left hip pocket.

Keeping her wrists locked together with his left hand, he slid his right hand down—down her arm, her left side, grazing her breast, to the top of her jeans. He watched her face the entire time, noting the way her lids fluttered under his touch. Needing proof that he wasn't the only one who could not control himself when they were together.

"Here?" he asked in a low voice, dipping his fingers inside her pocket.

"Mmm-hmm." Her lids fluttered closed as a sigh eased past her pretty lips.

He reached in, wriggling his fingers deeper into her tight pocket until he found something tucked at the very bottom. He pulled it out. Holding it close, he recognized his cuff link, and the sight brought back the night he'd spent at Daisy's. The thought caused his cock to harden. He tossed the cuff link onto his desk, the action creating a sense of déjà vu. He gazed down at her, seeing her as he'd seen her that night. Gorgeous. Sexy. Shy.

Dangerous.

"Is that it?" he asked, his free hand still playing around the seam of her pocket.

She blinked her eyes open. "No." She drew in a shaky breath and let it out again. Rolling her eyes toward the door, she said, "I recognize those guys." She grunted and shifted beneath him. He responded by leaning into her even more. "You invited them to the fund-raiser."

"So what if I did?" He moved his thigh back and forth between her parted legs.

"You didn't have to do that."

"No. I didn't." With a gentle upward motion, he ground into her with his knee. He could feel her heat through the material of her jeans and his shorts.

"Thank you."

She met his knee's upward movement with a downward gyration, which nearly killed him.

"You're a good guy, Jamie."

He was not a good guy. "Yeah," he said harshly. "I'm a regular Clark Kent."

With a throaty laugh she said, "Does that make me Lois Lane?"

Jamie didn't answer. When she tugged against his hold, as if trying to get away, it only played into his unwanted arousal. Oh, he was *so* not a good guy at the moment.

"Um, Jamie? Are you going to let me go?" Her lips remained in a pretty O shape after the word *go* and Jamie lost it. Her body was so soft. Her liquid eyes gazed up at him, large and full of desire. Her small, pink tongue darted out, wetting those kissable lips.

He gave in.

Dropping his head to her level, he swooped in, crushing her lips with his need. The softness of her mouth amped up his desire and frustration to the point that he couldn't decide whether he wanted to kiss her or push her away.

Her soft moan broke the spell and Jamie fell back, as if

the woman was a red-hot coal. "What am I doing?" Raising his hands above his head, he said, "I didn't mean to do that."

She frowned and touched her lips. "You didn't?"

"No." It was a lie. Of course he meant to do it. That and more. Much more.

"Felt like you meant it."

Backing away, he explained, "Sometimes I get this way. After a fight." It was partly true. The adrenaline from fighting could act as an aphrodisiac. But did adrenaline explain why he wanted to strip her and take her against the wall, hard? Did the thrill of the fight explain why he'd held her captive and still longed to do it again, except this time with her bare legs wrapped around his waist, her soft naked breasts against his chest? Did it explain how he longed to see her eyes grow hazy with desire as he pushed his cock inside her?

"Oh." The light in Daisy's eyes dimmed and she bit her lip. "In that case, I guess I'll be on my way."

"That's a good idea."

She skirted around him to the door. "Thanks again."

"Sure."

There. They were done. Now she could leave and the sooner she left and was out of his life, the sooner he could return to the ring and pound away the thing in his gut. The sooner his world could return to normal.

She straightened her shirt and looked him square in the eye, her delicate brows twitching in confusion. "Okay, then," she said. "Goodbye."

"Goodbye."

She stayed exactly where she was.

"You'd better go now, Daisy."

"Oh, right." She opened the door and then stood in the opening. "Goodbye."

"Do you need me to walk you to the door?"

"No." She still didn't leave.

"Daisy? Why are you still here?"

The way she nibbled her lip almost had Jamie dragging her back inside his office, slamming the door and giving in to his desire. Instead he clenched his fists.

"I just—"

"You just what?"

Shaking her head, she said, "Never mind. It's not important." Her chest rose with a big breath. "I guess I made a mess of everything." Her chin quivered, prompting her to cover her mouth, nod and turn away.

Jamie ground his teeth as he watched her leave. This was exactly what he needed to avoid. These emotional scenes. Every time with her it was out-of-control passion followed by a roller coaster of emotion. A recipe for disaster, the kind of thing he'd worked hard at avoiding all his adult life.

As she hurried toward the door, Jamie overheard one of the guys call out, "Next time you come, bring some of those cinnamon things."

"Yeah, and cheese buns."

"Apple strudel."

"She's not coming back," Jamie shouted to the gym at large. When a few of the men hollered back complaints, he yelled, "Men only."

Daisy turned at the door, and even from that distance, he could read the hurt on her face. He had to grip the door frame with both hands to keep himself from chasing her, apologizing and taking her into his arms.

He had to let her go. It was for the best. Daisy Sinclair deserved a man who would not let her down, and that man was not him.

JAMIE'S REACTION HURT and confused Daisy. She rode home in the back of the cab, staring out the window but seeing her reflection instead.

He's smitten with you. They were her mother's words but her grandmother's voice.

"If he's so smitten, why was he such a jerk?" she whispered to the reflection.

"Sorry, lady. Did you say something?" The driver asked.

"No," Daisy said, raising her voice over the loud hip-hop music. "Just talking to myself back here."

"You're not one of those crazies are you?"

"Sometimes, but not today." She winked at the driver, who was regarding her through the rearview mirror, then went back to gazing out the window. Staring at her reflection wasn't helping her figure out Jamie's reaction. If he really didn't want to see her again, why kiss her? If he really liked her, why had he been such an ass? None of it made sense.

Things were no clearer a few minutes later when the cab pulled up outside Nana Sin's. Right off, the building looked odd. Vacant. There was nothing left to identify it as the former bakery except the darkened patch on the brick where the sign had hung. The signs, the furniture, the equipment, all of it had been packed, loaded and moved to the storage facility. Everything gone in one day.

It was completely surreal.

On the front door was a new sign explaining the closure, though she'd have to post a different one tomorrow as this one was covered in handwritten condolences and lamentations over the closing of the shop, including a scrawled note that read, *You are the best and I will miss you more than you'll ever know.* Johnny.

Unlocking the door to the apartment entrance, Daisy slowly climbed the steps. How many more times would she get to do this? She paused and put a hand against the wall, feeling woozy all of a sudden. Her new apartment was vacant and she'd been told she could move in immediately, but she wasn't ready. Not even close.

Maybe she'd do some painting over at the new place while it was empty, something bright and cheery, because she planned on being bright and cheery.

Someday.

She opened the door at the top of the stairs and looked around her home as if seeing it for the first time. The apartment was small but it was cozy—though in her hunt for places, Daisy had realized that *cozy* was code word for teeny-tiny. A brick fireplace, crown molding, original fixtures. It was a great place.

A great place that would soon no longer be hers, as the boxes lined up against the wall served to remind her.

This was it. Regardless if she stayed a couple days or until the very last day of possession, nothing was going to be the same again, and Daisy experienced a tingling sensation, starting at the crown of her head and fluttering down her body, as though she'd been showered in glass dust.

It's impossible to feel blue with the smell of fresh baking in a kitchen.

"Are you going to keep talking to me when I move?" Daisy asked the room in general. Of course no one answered. Daisy was ninety per cent sure the voice she heard wasn't really her grandmother but simply memories surfacing, probably because she was surrounded by the place where the memories were created. But real or imagined, sane or semischizoid, the voice was comforting, and Daisy didn't want it to stop.

Sitting down at her kitchen table, Daisy traced the wood grain on the old table. "I don't know what to do," she muttered to herself. "I just don't know what to do."

Out of nowhere, her stove dinged. It did that sometimes. The electrical was wonky in the old building, lights cutting in and out, appliances shutting off and on, but Daisy decided to take it as a sign. She knew exactly what she needed to do. Jumping to her feet, she turned the oven on to three hundred fifty, unpacked her baking supplies and proceeded to empty her cupboard of ingredients: flour, sugar, butter, salt...

Rolling up her sleeves, Daisy organized her things on the counter, the simple act already starting to make her feel better.

AFTER SPENDING THE day painting the kitchen of her new apartment—lemon yellow, which made the place feel lovely and sunshiny—Daisy headed back to the old apartment to pack the cinnamon buns into boxes of four. She loaded the boxes into two large shopping bags and toted them down to the curb outside. Her first few attempts to flag a cab failed but a few minutes later, one finally stopped. When she ducked down to give the address, she realized it was the same driver she'd had last night.

"Hey, lady," he said with a grin. "Feeling crazy today?"

Putting the bags in first, Daisy climbed in after. "I haven't decided yet. You?"

"I'm all good." His chuckle was deep and infectious, and Daisy found herself laughing along with him.

For the duration of the ride, she reflected on the fact that in spite of everything going on, she felt better today. Lighter. Was it painting her new apartment? The act of baking? The prospect of giving her baking away?

Daisy didn't know, but she decided to accept the reprieve for whatever it was. It felt good to feel good. Smiling, she glanced forward and caught the driver watching her in the rearview mirror again. She waved.

"I know you."

Daisy leaned forward. "Uh…you gave me a ride last night, remember?"

"No, I mean you're the baking lady. You were all over the news last week." He lifted his nose and sniffed the air. "Smells like you got something good in those bags."

"As a matter of fact, I do."

"How about doing a hungry brother a solid? Because damn, crazy baking lady, whatever you got in there smells goo-ood."

When they pulled over in front of the gym, Daisy took one of the boxes out of the bag and gave it to the driver with her fare. "Take some home to your family."

"Thanks, lady." He got out and opened the door for her. "Do you need help with that?"

"Nope. I can manage, thanks."

Daisy climbed the steps to the gym, her heart beating erratically, her palms damp where she held the handles of the bags, her tummy doing gymnastics, twists, flips and somersaults. She tried the door, but of course it was locked, and this time there was no one to let her in. She noticed a small buzzer to the right of the door, pressed it and waited until eventually someone came. This time when she looked up and saw Colin Forsythe, she didn't mistake him for Jamie and, in fact, marveled at the fact that she'd ever confused the two. They were so different.

"We were taking bets as to who forgot his key this time. *You* were not in the running." He opened the door wide for her to come in.

Daisy made her way into the gym and was greeted by cheers from the guys. She held the bags aloft. "Who wants cinnamon buns?" There was a big, manly stampede, and Daisy grabbed one of the boxes before they were all gone.

"If you're looking for Jamie," Colin said, "he's in his office."

"Oh, thanks." Squaring her shoulders, Daisy made her way past the ring—where the two men who'd been sparring stopped to yell at the others to save them some of the buns. She could do this. This was a test. She had to know whether Jamie had feelings for her or not. His bad behavior yesterday seemed to indicate not, but the searing heat of his kiss said the opposite. She pressed her fingertips to her lips as she stood outside his closed door and then called, "Special delivery," as she knocked.

Jamie opened the door, much like his twin had done a few minutes ago. Yep, there were so many differences. Jamie was bigger, broader across the shoulders. His face wider, his eyes sparkling with irreverence—though not so much right now.

Clearing her throat, Daisy presented the box, a peace offering. She noted the way his nostrils flared as he took a deep breath. For a second, she thought he might turn away without accepting her gift, but a loud rumbling from his stomach seemed to make him change his mind.

"Thank you." He took the box without a smile.

So Daisy smiled wide enough for both of them. "You're welcome." Then she turned and walked away. "See you," she called over her shoulder.

Was he watching her? Should she check? Daisy paused. No. Let him keep guessing. She kept walking, though she might have been swaying her hips a little more than usual, and she couldn't keep the satisfied smirk off her face when she heard Jamie's door slam a few seconds later. As she neared the area where she'd dropped off the bags, Colin caught up to her. "What do we owe you for all of this?"

"Nothing." She glanced back toward Jamie's closed office. "But I'm bringing my gym clothes tomorrow. Someone is going to teach me how to use that." She pointed at the big, heavy bag Owen was currently pummeling.

Colin laughed. "You've got game, girl. But I warn you, my brother can be an idiot sometimes."

"Funny," Daisy said with a playful wink, "he's said the same thing about you."

16

GOD, WHAT A DAY. After spending the morning interviewing candidates to replace his partner Carson, Jamie had worked through lunch, trying to catch up on his files. And then, in the afternoon he'd received a panicked call from his client Chloe. Despite the protective order that was in place, her ex had broken into the house again.

Through it all, Daisy Sinclair was never far from his thoughts. He'd blink and see her face, her expressive eyes, her luscious lips. He'd walk down the hall and hear a woman's voice and it'd be Daisy's telling him, *You're a good guy, Jamie.* He'd close his eyes because of the insistent pounding in his temples and be accosted by a vision of Daisy, naked on her bed, beckoning to him.

Now, a rumbling unease stewed in the pit of his stomach. He considered going home instead of to the gym tonight, but he really needed the gym. Plus, Daisy's box of buns sat unopened in his kitchen and would be a cruel reminder of what he wanted but couldn't have.

So the gym it was. He needed to let loose on someone. Or allow someone to let loose on him. Didn't matter, really. Being in the ring was the only time he could let go. Forget.

Ease the guilt of what he hadn't been able to do. For his clients, for his sister. For Daisy.

The second he opened the door, he knew something was wrong. It was too quiet. There was no one in the ring. No one at the weight benches. No loud, pounding bass from the speakers. Stepping farther into the space, Jamie saw the crowd surrounding the heavy bags.

Then he heard her voice, and the restless thing pacing like a caged animal in the pit of his stomach suddenly pounced at the bars.

"Take that!" Daisy cried, followed by a cheer from the spectators.

Quietly Jamie approached the throng.

"And that!" Hoots and hollers followed Daisy's show. She grinned at the men. "This is fun."

Jamie inserted himself into the group surrounding the bag. Daisy was suited up, wearing much-too-snug workout clothes. Her short shorts showed off her shapely legs and her fine ass. A tight yoga top accentuated the cleavage of her full breasts, her narrow waist and her curvy hips.

"No more!" She jabbed twice at the bag.

"Go girl! Give it all you got."

A cross and an upper cut had her hair and other parts of her bouncing with enthusiasm.

"Let 'em have it, Daisy."

"God, you're so cute when you're mad."

Did she honestly have no idea how she looked right now? Did she not realize she was surrounded by raging testosterone?

With a series of pretty grunts, Daisy let her fists fly, reminding Jamie—oh, so vividly—of their time together in the ring. The bars gave way, freeing the dangerous predator that dwelled in his gut.

He strode up between the bag and Daisy. The group went silent.

In a low voice he said, "Out." He met every single one of the men's eyes individually, conveying his displeasure. His dominance. His ownership. "All of you. Get out."

"WHAT DID YOU do that for?" Daisy demanded, tossing the gloves to the floor so she could rest her hands on her hips. The last of the men filed out of the gym, some throwing back halfhearted complaints, others elbowing each other, sharing knowing glances.

"Get dressed, Daisy."

She glanced down at herself. "I am dressed."

Striding to the wall where there was a water cooler and a shelf stacked with towels, Jamie grabbed a towel and tossed it at her. "You are basically in your underwear."

"These are workout clothes. My underwear is *way* more revealing." She threw the towel back at him. "Of course, you should know that. Or have you forgotten?"

"I have *not* forgotten." His voice was so low it was lethal.

Daisy gulped. She'd never seen him like this. His face was red, as though he'd been in the ring, but he hadn't, because he'd just arrived. His normally full lips were pulled back into a thin line and his jaw was rigid with tension. When he took a step toward her, she found herself automatically taking a step back.

"Why do you keep coming here?"

She sidestepped around one of the big bags, pushing it toward him as if that would stop him. "Why do you think?"

He caught the bag and held it. "Don't answer a question with a question."

She threw her hands up. "Then don't ask a stupid question."

His gaze narrowed. "Are you trying to drive me crazy?"

"No." Daisy knew she was the world's worst liar. Her expression always gave her away, and Jamie called her on it.

"Don't lie."

She glanced over her shoulder, backing in another direction, trying another tactic. "How can I drive you crazy? You'd actually have to care about me for that to happen."

"You know I care about you."

"No. I don't. Because you're kind of acting like an ass right now and maybe even scaring me a little bit."

He flinched as though she'd slapped him, but that didn't stop his slow, steady stalking of her. "Good. You need to be scared a little bit." He pounced, grabbing her arms and tugging her up against him. "You are way too trusting."

She shook her head. "Trusting is good."

His grip tightened. "No. Trusting is bad. This is a bad part of town, and for all you know, these are bad guys."

She shook her head no.

His searing gaze swept down her body and back up. "You have no idea how good you look." He took a deep breath. "How great you smell." His lids slid to half-mast. "You think you're tempting them with your baking?" One hand went around to the back of her neck and he tilted her head up to him. "*You* are the temptation, Daisy. You." His other hand slid down to her ass and he pulled her snug against his big, hard body. "And it's too much for me."

Daisy wound her arms around his neck. "Good," she whispered, standing on her tiptoes so she could look him in the eye. "Then stop fighting it."

First he made a sound deep in his chest, a growly, savage sound. Then his mouth descended on hers, needy, hungry, possessive. She kissed him back, equally needy, equally hungry. He'd been right about the arousing effects of boxing, because she was more aroused now than she could ever remember feeling…except for that time with Jamie in the ring.

"What is this thing between us?" he asked, sounding as if he was in pain.

"I don't know," she whispered against his lips. Tasting him, letting him suck her tongue into his mouth, opening her mouth so she could suck on him.

He backed her up to the ring and lifted her to sit on the edge so she was level with him, the bottom rope at the back of her head. He nudged her legs apart and stepped between them. "It's out of control."

"I know."

He held on to her face with both hands, having his way with her mouth. Nipping and biting, plunging with his tongue, sweeping with a thoroughness she'd never experienced, as if he had to taste every part of her.

"You should hate me," he murmured.

"I kind of did."

His fingers threaded through her hair, gripping in a wonderfully intense way. "Then why are you here?"

"I can't stay away." She gave her hands permission to tug on his shirt and roam underneath. She loved this part of him, the band of soft hair around his navel, his warm skin over solid, rippling muscles.

He nuzzled the skin beneath her jaw. "You told me it was over."

"I know."

"Do you want it to be over?"

"No." She let her head fall back, loving the feel of his lips on her throat, the stubble of his beard rough against her jaw. "Do you?"

He lapped at her neck, smelling her damp skin as he went. "I don't know." He pulled away. "I should, but…"

"But what?"

"I can't stop wanting you."

"Then don't."

He groaned and lifted her down from the ring. Pressing his forehead against hers, he whispered, "I wish I could, Daisy. I'm not good for you."

"Says who?"

He gazed down into her eyes, his pupils large and dark, making his eyes appear almost black. Tortured.

"Me."

"Don't I get a say?"

His nostrils flared, and Daisy swore he was taking in her scent. "You're too trusting."

"I want you, Jamie. I've always wanted you. Even when I hated you, I wanted you."

Discomfort flashed across his face, followed quickly by something else. Resignation? Desire?

"I want to make love to you," she said.

He sucked in a breath. "Not here."

"Where?"

He caressed her cheek with the back of his knuckles. "Your place."

She shook her head. "It's in chaos. I was planning to stay with Gloria tonight."

He frowned, silently searching her face, as if he was looking for the answer to a question he'd never asked. She touched his swollen mouth, so much better than the thin angry line from before. "You should take me home right now, Jamie. Or—"

"Or what?"

She kissed him, rubbing his delicious erection through his pants. "Or we're going to be using that emergency condom right now, and you're going to do me right here, whether you want to or not."

JAMIE DROVE LIKE a demon. His body was on fire. That's what Daisy did to him. She lit him on fire until he quickly burned out of control. Oh, he'd tried to do the right thing, keep her at arm's length, but for whatever reason, he was unable to be rational around the woman.

Once parked in his underground spot, he helped Daisy off the bike and took her hand as he led her to the elevator that would take them up to his apartment. The other reason he was feeling so out of control was that he'd never brought a woman here before.

Ever.

He'd always claimed that it was for the women's benefit. They were more at home in their own places with all their toiletries on hand. But the truth was he liked to be the one to call the shots, have control over when things ended, when he could leave. He preferred to keep a certain distance and that meant keeping women out of his space.

Now here he was bringing Daisy Sinclair into his inner sanctuary, and he couldn't wait to get her there.

"Can I get you something to drink?" he asked after unlocking the door and letting her inside.

"Water, please. That workout made me thirsty." Jamie felt the weird combination of anger and attraction resurface at the memory of Daisy putting on a sultry, sexy boxing show for all the men.

God.

"Ice?"

"Yes, please." As he prepared her water, Daisy explored his apartment, running her fingertips along the shelves, the spines of books, picking up picture frames and setting them down again. "Um, Jamie?"

"Yeah?" He came to join her in the living room.

She pointed to the three pictures on his mantel. "Were you married?"

All three were of Sarah, two of her by herself, one with the three siblings. Funny. He'd never even considered what those pictures might imply to someone who didn't know him. "No. That's my sister."

"Ah." Daisy picked up his favorite, Sarah with her golden retriever puppy, Gordon. "She's really pretty. Does she live in Chicago?"

Jamie passed Daisy the glass, took the picture from her hand and studied it for a second. "She died."

"Oh, I'm so sorry. When did that happen?"

"My fourth year of law school." He replaced the picture. "Eight years ago."

Daisy set her water down. She didn't speak, didn't ask what happened. She simply wrapped her arms around his waist and rested her head against his chest. She stayed there, just breathing, just being there.

After a while, she pressed a hand to his chest. "You have a Celtic symbol on your chest, over your heart."

"I do."

"Is it—"

"For her? Yes."

"I wondered." She rubbed a circle over the spot.

Jamie took her hand and kissed her palm. She placed it flat against his cheek, stroking the side of his face, his whiskers, gazing up at him, her eyes bright with compassion, comforting him in a way that he hadn't known he needed to be comforted.

He took her hand in his. "Come with me."

17

JAMIE'S HAND WAS warm in hers as he led her down the hall to his bedroom. He had a nice apartment. Comfortable, modern, stylishly furnished. Gloria would approve of the feng-shui-ness of it all. Yet there was something off, and Daisy could feel it.

A sadness, maybe?

When she'd asked about Sarah, Jamie's whole demeanor changed. If she could see energy—which she couldn't—she'd have seen him shut down, shut off, leaving her feeling cold and lonely.

So Daisy had done the only thing she could think of to do. She'd put her head against his chest and listened to his heart. It beat strong and fierce inside his chest, and when his hands tangled in her curls in the way she loved, she knew it was going to be okay. The unbearable passion they'd both felt at the gym had abated, but in its place was something softer, gentler, more compassionate…something better.

Once inside his bedroom, Jamie turned her around in his arms, sifting his fingers through her curls before leaning down to kiss her. It wasn't the relentless kiss of earlier. It was gentler, his tongue questing softly against her lips, dancing with hers, a lovely, slow waltz in which he led and she followed. The clothes he'd made her put on before they left the gym soon fell away again. Daisy didn't know how it happened. There was no ripping, tearing or grappling—just a simple shedding of outer garments that fell like gentle rain to the ground.

"You are so beautiful," he whispered, gazing down at her naked body, his voice rough, catching a little on the word *so*.

For whatever bizarre reason, tears sprang to her eyes and she looked away, but Jamie took hold of her chin and turned her back to face him. Though his expression was perplexed, he didn't ask and she didn't offer an explanation for her tears. If he wanted her to stop crying, however, he shouldn't have blotted her tears with his thumb and then brought his thumb to his lips to kiss, because that action just increased the flow. Shuddering through her breath, Daisy nuzzled closer to him, kissing his throat, moving down to his chest and placing a soft kiss over his heart while sliding a hand lower to where his cock grew between them.

She squeezed. "I love this part of you," she said, her voice on the ragged side.

"Good. Because that part of me loves you." He shifted his stance. "Particularly what you're doing right now."

Chuckling through her tears, Daisy met Jamie's gaze.

Wow.

If she'd doubted his feelings before, the way he was gazing at her now answered any questions she'd had. His dark chocolate eyes shone with tenderness and desire. Never breaking his gaze, she slowly dropped to her knees, sliding her hands down his muscled thighs as she went. It wasn't until she was kneeling right before him and she used the side of her cheek to caress his leg and then the length of his cock that she broke their gaze. Closing her eyes, she inhaled deeply, breathing in his masculine scent, exploring the texture of his shaft with the side of her face.

He groaned.

She rubbed his head across her mouth, the moisture from his tip glossing her already moist lips.

"You are going to be the death of me."

"I hope not." She tilted her head back. Holy, it was a long way up there. His grip in her hair intensified as she leaned forward and took just the head of him in her mouth.

"Daisy."

She liked hearing her name said that way. It made her feel wanton and powerful. Holding him firmly in her hand, she dipped lower in order to suck him in deeper, hollowing her cheeks around him as she withdrew.

His groan was almost as good as the sound of her name, and when he hauled her to her feet so he could have his way with her mouth, she felt liquid with desire.

"I have never met a woman like you," Jamie said as he did that other thing she loved so much, picked her up—easily—and placed her on the bed.

Jamie crawled onto the bed with her, moving on top of her. "You're under my skin, you know that?" The muscles of his shoulders appeared more massive than ever as he held himself aloft above her. "I tried to stop thinking about you." He dipped low to nip her lip. "But you've got this hold on me."

"It's mutual." Daisy ran her hands over those shoulders, marveling at his strength, and then down his equally muscular back. She'd never been with a man who had such big muscles. They were lovely.

Slowly he lowered his body to hers. She made room for him by parting her thighs and bending her knees, opening herself to him, rubbing herself against him in a way that she hoped would tell him how ready she was for this. But Jamie was being too careful, moving in slow circles between her thighs, trying not to crush her with his weight.

Didn't he know Daisy wanted his weight? Wanted to be crushed? She wanted him everywhere at once, on her, in her, his body, his mouth, his tongue, his cock. All of it. "Please, Jamie," she said, grabbing hold of his hips and drawing him close. "Please."

He kissed the "please" right out of her mouth, holding her tongue captive until she forgot how to speak. He paused in his assault on her mouth to reach for something beside the bed, a small plastic square. When had he put the condom there? She didn't know and quite frankly didn't care. "May I?" she said, holding her hand out for the plastic wrapper.

"Since you asked so nicely." His lips twisted up on the left as he handed it to her.

She tore it open with her teeth and pulled the slick rubber out of the sleeve while Jamie straightened his arms to hold himself above her. Those arms of his were to die for. She nearly became distracted by them—they might just be her favorite part of him—but when the heavy head of his cock twitched against her mound, as if in anticipation of what she was about to do, her focus was on that wonderfully male part of him and that part alone. He was so big. So hard... Mmm, this was a favorite part of him, too.

She rolled the lubed rubber over him, holding the base of his shaft firmly in her fist, and then guided him to her parted legs.

"Seriously, Daisy," he said gruffly, glancing down at his erection. "That felt so good, I think you're going to have to do it every time."

"Every time?" Why did those words thrill Daisy to her core? Maybe because even though she was in the middle of this, she knew it would end and she didn't want it to. She wanted it never to end. She wanted to be here like this with Jamie as often as she could.

Holding on to him, she lifted her pelvis and guided him along her damp slit, rubbing his wide head against her swollen nub, back and forth, in and out. Yes. So good. So very, very good. "I love how you feel."

"Me, too." Jamie caressed the side of her face. "And while I enjoy being your personal sex toy—" he removed her hand from his cock, replacing it with his "—I need to be inside you."

While holding her gaze, he thrust, seating himself inside of her fully. Daisy arched and cried out. How was it possible that his body filled hers so perfectly? How could something so strange—fitting two bodies together—feel so wonderful? She wrapped her legs around his waist, needing him as close and deep as physically possible.

"Oh, Daisy." Jamie pulled out only to slam back inside again. "I've missed you."

"Mmm." She held on to him, holding him flush, wanting him to stay exactly where he was, filling her completely, making her feel whole. "I've missed you, too."

He pulled back again and she gasped from the loss, only to pound home, and she cried out in welcome. What a wonder. What a thing to have his body so close, so deep, so excruciatingly good.

Jamie pulled out of her and grasped hold of her hips and lifted. "Turn over. I need you on your hands and knees."

Oh, yes. That was exactly what she needed, too. Only thing was, her arms were not exactly in favor of supporting her at the moment, and Daisy had to make do by resting on her elbows.

Jamie didn't seem to mind.

"Woman, you have a gorgeous ass." He caressed her bottom roughly, grabbing the globes of her ass and then palming the warmth of her exposed pussy. "Do you have any idea what you do to me?" He groaned, and before Daisy could reply, his mouth was feasting on her.

"Jamie!" she cried, her body alight with tingles and sparkles. Though his mouth was marvelous, she missed the fullness of his heavy flesh inside her. "Jamie, please," she begged.

With one last lap of his tongue, he surfaced, digging his fingers into the flesh at her hips. "You taste so good. So, so good."

She wagged her ass at him, desperate to be filled. "Please," she whispered to the pillow in front of her.

Whether Jamie heard her or not, it didn't matter, because he found her and impaled her and sent her to that place between heaven and hell, pleasure and pain, where everything was wonderful and confusing and Daisy didn't know if she was up or down, coming or going. His body moved inside hers as his fingers strummed her most sensitive flesh, creating a symphony of sensation, clashing cymbals, trumpeting horns, screeching violins…

Crying out in ecstasy as she came, hard and thorough, convulsing within Jamie's embrace. The last thing she heard before collapsing was Jamie's moan of ultimate pleasure in her ear.

THEY SAT AT his breakfast counter drinking coffee… together. This morning she'd heated up the cinnamon buns from the box—not commenting on the fact that the box hadn't been opened unless a raised eyebrow counted as a comment—and made a fruit salad from the contents in his fridge. He read the newspaper, as was his morning routine, and Daisy did a crossword from a magazine.

"What's a six-letter word for ornery?"

"Crabby," Jamie replied absently.

"Needs to start with *G*."

"Grouchy."

"That's seven."

"Grumpy."

"Ooh! That works."

Jamie raised his head and smiled. Then he frowned because having Daisy there, doing a crossword puzzle all familiar-like while he drank his coffee, was all wrong.

Except that it felt so right.

So had her warm, naked body this morning. So had her warm, naked body last night.

She looked up, probably having felt him staring at her. Her delicate brows drew together. "Everything okay?"

"Yep."

"Great." She chewed on the end of the pencil. "Can I ask a favor?"

"Sure."

"It's just…the new place still smells like paint and the other is all packed up and it's hard to bake over there…" Her brow crinkled, a wave of sadness washing over her. She shook her head and the sadness was gone. "Can I use your kitchen today?"

"Sure. I'll leave you a key." The words were out before he could take them back. Was he insane? He'd already broken the rule of having a woman stay over and now he was giving her his key?

"Thanks." Her smile lit the room. "I was planning chocolate-fudge brownies. Do you think the guys would prefer them with nuts or without?" She played with a curl, thinking. "I'll probably make both—"

"No." The word burst out of him, hot and possessive.

"No nuts?"

Jamie folded the paper, slowly, carefully, needing control, because the idea of Daisy going back over to the gym after her sexy, seminaked boxing display last night drove him to the brink of sanity. "You're not taking any more baking over to *the guys*."

She sat back, crossing her arms over her chest. "Aah, you're not the boss of me. You know that, right?"

"My place, my gym, my rules." He ground his teeth to refrain from saying more.

She cocked her head to one side, her wonderfully messy curls bouncing playfully in juxtaposition to her angry expression. "That's stupid."

"It's not stupid, Daisy. It's safe."

She stood, walked up to him and gave him a little shove on the shoulder. "Just because we've slept together doesn't mean you own me. If you don't want me baking here, I'll just go to Gloria's."

"That's probably a good idea."

Her eyes grew cloudy. "So...you don't want me to use your kitchen?"

"I didn't say that."

"What did you say?"

"I said to stay away from the gym."

"Why? I thought the guys at the gym were your friends."

"They are."

"So how is it not safe for me to go there?" This time she jabbed him on the shoulder.

Jamie stared her down, daring her to push him further. "They may be my friends, but they are still men. Big, aggressive, occasionally violent men with way too much testosterone coursing through their veins."

"Exactly. Those guys eat a lot."

He curled his fingers around the paper. "And you, Daisy, are a beautiful, funny, charming woman who has this innocent—"

Her gasp cut him off. "You think I'm beautiful and

funny?" Her smile reached all the way up into her sparkling eyes.

"Of course I do, but that's not—"

Her eyes grew even wider. "You get jealous when the guys pay attention to me." She sucked in a breath, just realizing something. "That's why you were so weird yesterday."

"It wasn't jealousy. It was..." Jamie paused. If not jealousy, then what? Protectiveness? Possessiveness? How could he explain to Daisy that he couldn't stand the idea of her getting into trouble? That it was simply instinct to do everything in his power to keep anything bad from happening to her? Even if that bad thing was him?

She smiled coyly. "Jamie Forsythe, are you in love with me?"

Her question took him completely by surprise because of both the cheekiness of her tone and the question itself. He sputtered a nonsensical response.

She rubbed his arm. "Don't worry. Your secret's safe with me."

"There's no secret, Daisy. I'm not."

"You're not what?"

"What you just said."

She squinted at him. "Can't you say it?"

The woman was playing him; her saucy smile gave her away. But regardless of the fact that this was nothing more than a verbal sparring match, the conversation was making Jamie twitchy. "Of course I can say it."

"Then say it."

"What? That I'm in love with you?"

She covered her mouth, but her hand did nothing to hide the awful mixture of mirth and delight glowing in her eyes.

"Daisy." Jamie said her name quietly as a means of gaining control of this situation. If he was muddled this morning, it was because she was still here and she shouldn't be, though the idea of her spending her nights anywhere else was unpalatable. "Let's not get ahead of ourselves."

"I'm teasing, Jamie." She continued to rub his arm—which felt so nice, Jamie didn't want her to stop—but eventually her expression grew serious as she watched her hand moving up and down the length of his bicep.

She raised her gaze, all joking gone. "But let's get something straight. Baking is what I do. I've done it every day of my life."

"I know."

"I don't do it for me, Jamie. I do it for others, and I'm not about to stop now, not even if you say so…" Wickedness returned in the form of a sweetly crinkled nose. "Not even if you're in love with me."

He was about to deny her claim again, but stopped himself because he realized, by the secret smile she didn't bother to hide, that she was baiting him. She glanced up from her crossword puzzle and winked—cheeky woman—before going back to it, or at least, pretending to.

He hid his smile behind his newspaper. That's what he *liked* about Daisy; her playfulness and…pretty much everything else.

Did he love her?

He doubted it, not that he had an accurate gauge of the emotion. He'd never been in love before.

What Jamie did know was that he cared for Daisy more than any woman he'd ever met and the realization left him feeling both comforted and terrified.

18

THE MUSIC WAS on loud—Jamie had a really nice sound system—as they cooked together in his kitchen. Even though Daisy had spent the entire afternoon in his kitchen, it was still an unfamiliar space, and it was nice to have Jamie there to help. Actually, he was more than helping, he was co-cooking, which was a bit of a surprise given how weird he'd been this morning. Hot then cold. Then lukewarm. There was a moment this morning when she wondered if she'd gone too far with the teasing, but based on the way he'd kissed her goodbye and left her the key to his place, she figured he was okay with it.

Now, she was busy toasting cloves, a cinnamon stick, anise and coriander for the mole sauce while Jamie was taking care of the chicken. To be accurate, he was neglecting the chicken as he sidled up behind her, as if this morning's weirdness had never happened, and rested his hands on her hips. He leaned his head over her shoulder, drawing in a deep breath.

"That smells delicious."

Daisy closed her eyes. She had to agree that the spices were deliciously fragrant, but Jamie's body pressed up behind hers? That was even more delicious.

"Can you seed those chili peppers?" she asked, wriggling her ass against his front.

He groaned in her ear. "You play dirty, woman. Appealing to my two most basic appetites at the same time."

"You love it." She tilted her head up and to the side, presenting her lips for a kiss, which Jamie gave her with enthusiasm, making her temporarily forget the food on the stove. With a playful elbow to his midriff, she nudged Jamie away. "Get back to work, slacker."

He chuckled and stepped away, grabbing the wine bottle to refill each of their glasses. Daisy couldn't remember feeling happier. Was there anything better than cooking a sexy meal with a sexy man, with the promise of sex afterward? She stole a peek at Jamie.

Nope.

Her tummy rumbled pleasantly at the prospect of both the meal and the man. It had been a pretty much perfect day so far. She'd spent the day in Jamie's kitchen baking cheese buns, rye bread, raisin bread and double chocolate-chip cookies, all items requested by the Families in Need Shelter. When Jamie came home to a kitchen full of bread and learned of her intention to head downtown to the shelter to drop off the fruits of her labor, he'd insisted on accompanying her.

"Jamie, I'm a big girl and—"

"I know." He took her hands. "I know you are capable of taking care of yourself. I'm asking you do to this for me, for my benefit." He glanced toward his mantel. "For my peace of mind."

Funny how when he put it like that, Daisy was happy to oblige him, and she was also happy for the help. After dropping everything off, they'd stopped at the market on the way back and gotten all the ingredients for one of her favorite meals, chicken in mole sauce made the traditional way with fresh spices, raisins, almonds, pumpkin seeds and chilies, blended with corn tortillas to thicken the sauce and finished with melted Mexican chocolate.

Heavenly.

An hour and a half later, they were seated side by side at Jamie's dining room table and already on their second bottle of wine, laughing like a couple of giddy teenagers.

"Allow me." Jamie cut into his chicken, making sure there was ample sauce, and held the fork up to her mouth.

Daisy parted her lips, guiding the fork inside with her tongue. She softly closed her lips around the morsel, breathing in as she tasted. "Mmm." God, that was good, and the flavor was enhanced by Jamie's enjoyment of watching her eat. Once she swallowed, she copied his actions, carving a piece of meat, dipping it in sauce and feeding him.

His eyes rolled back inside his skull as he moved the food around in his mouth. Once he'd finished his bite, a devilishly seductive smile grew as he studied her. "I'm not surprised this is your favorite dish."

Daisy shrugged. "Any entree that includes chocolate is pretty much a given."

He leaned forward and kissed her, his lips still flavored with mole. "Perfectly sweet and spicy. Lusty and rich, it's the flavor of sunshine and happiness."

Wow. That was it. Mole chicken tasted like happiness. The thought occurred to her that Jamie should have been the food critic instead of Colin, and then the thought passed. Jamie was gazing into her eyes as he ate another piece, and there was a world of communication in his intense stare.

His guard was down, his fondness was clear and his intentions were wickedly obvious. "You know what else is perfectly sweet and spicy?"

Daisy shook her head.

"You." He yanked her chair close so that she was facing him and his knees were on either side of hers. "You're so incredibly sweet." He dipped a finger in his sauce and smeared it across her lips—a rather uncouth but terribly sexy maneuver. "But spicy, too." He leaned close and licked the sauce right off her mouth.

She groaned, opening so that his tongue could enter her mouth. How was it possible to meet a man who shared the same passion for flavor? Who found a sauce sexy?

"You taste like sunshine." He kissed her again. "You are the flavor of happiness."

Breath snagged in Daisy's throat, both because of his words and his expressive gaze. She blinked away the emotion his commentary created and swiped her own finger through the mound of sauce, holding it dripping up to Jamie's mouth. He parted his lips and drew her finger inside, sucking greedily at her sauce-covered digit. The sensation sent a thrill up her arm to the back of her throat.

"More."

She dipped two fingers this time. Her nostrils flared as she sucked in oxygen that suddenly seemed in short supply. Jamie held her hand in place, sucking her deep while running his tongue up and between her fingers.

Oh, God. It felt so good.

Never breaking eye contact, Jamie dared to undo the buttons on her blouse. If it hadn't been for the fact that her fingers were covered in mole, Daisy would have helped him, though he certainly didn't seem to need help as her blouse fluttered to the floor. Pulling Daisy to her feet, he gazed down at her, slipping a finger beneath the lace of her chocolate bra.

"You have the nicest underwear." He slid the straps off her shoulders and kissed the spot where one had been while his hands snaked around to undo the clasp.

"Umm, Jamie." Daisy sighed, her hands resting on his shoulders. "What are you doing?"

"This." He backed her up to the empty side of the table, lifted her to a sitting position on the edge and gently pushed her onto her back.

Daisy couldn't speak. She could barely breathe as Jamie slid a plate closer, dragged a finger through the sauce and painted her nipples in mole. Her head lolled against the hard wooden surface as Jamie lapped the dark sauce from one nipple before sucking the other right into his mouth. The mixture of Jamie's warm mouth and the chilies in the sauce made her nipples tingle in a way that caused intense pleasure to radiate across her chest and pool low in her abdomen. She arched up into his mouth, grasping his hair as he made a meal of her body.

"Daisy…" He moaned as he squeezed her breast, kissing and licking her flesh. Biting and sucking, crawling up onto the table so that he was right on top of her. "I've never… I've never…" He didn't finish because his mouth was now fused to hers, hot and hungry.

Daisy raked her fingers through his hair, just as hungry, just as needy, shifting beneath him as she tried to get comfortable on the hard surface. When Jamie tore his mouth away and then rolled off her, she cried out in displeasure. "Why are you stopping?"

He held his hand out to help her up. "Because I don't want to hurt you. So I'm taking you to the bathroom, where I'm going to take your clothes off, clean this sauce off you and make love to you. Then we're coming back out here to enjoy this meal."

IT WAS STRANGE how easy it was to fall into a routine with Daisy. Waking up to her soft, inviting body in the morning. Showering together, which usually resulted in them hurrying back to the bedroom to finish what they inevitably started in the shower. Showering again—independently— so that he wouldn't be tempted by Daisy's sweet form, while Daisy fixed some marvelous fare for breakfast.

After work he'd come home to a kitchen counter full of baking, they'd deliver it to whatever shelter or mission Daisy had arranged to take it to that day—there were so many in the city—and then they'd stop at the market to buy ingredients for the evening meal, which they'd cook together. It was becoming a bit of a test to see how far they'd make it into the meal before dashing off to the bedroom. It was never very far, and considering how much time they spent on cooking the food, he thought they really should try to eat a meal while it was hot one of these days.

He chuckled to himself as he straddled his bike. Despite the files piled in his inbox, he hadn't stayed late at work one night this week. Nor had he been to the gym in the last four days. The reason? He was too eager to get home to Daisy. She was the sexiest, most desirable woman he'd ever met. Sure, she was his type, curvy and luscious. Lusty and fun. But it was so much more that that. She had the sweetest spirit, she was kind and funny and giving and unpredictable, and he'd never thought he'd ever look forward to coming home to a woman the way he looked forward to coming home to Daisy. He'd never thought he'd want to share his space and life with someone the way he wanted to share them with Daisy. Even after such a short time, he couldn't imagine it any other way.

He didn't want it any other way.

So his disappointment at finding his apartment empty when he arrived home solidified the fact that he was more than smitten with Daisy Sinclair. Even the sight of her name in the contact list on his phone brought a stupid smile to his face. "I've got it bad," he muttered to himself as he dialed her number, needing to hear her voice.

Now.

"Where are you?" he asked after she'd barely said hello.

"I'm at my new place."

A sharp pain speared him between the ribs. Of course. What had he been thinking? This living arrangement was temporary.

"Did you hear me?"

Jamie rubbed his brow. "Sorry, what did you say?"

"The movers came today. Do you want to come over and take a look?"

With a glance around the apartment, which already felt empty without Daisy in it, Jamie said, "Of course. I'll be right there."

DAISY WONDERED IF she'd always feel like this—the little flippity-flops in her tummy—whenever she heard Jamie's voice. She buzzed him in and waited at the top of the stairs, wiping her damp palms on the front of her skirt.

She opened the door to him and had to hold onto the frame to keep herself upright. Jamie's infectious smile nearly knocked her off her feet.

"I missed you," he said, ducking low to kiss her smack on the lips.

"Missed you, too. But I've been busy. Moving day's a bitch."

"Why didn't you tell me it was moving day? I could have taken a vacation day to help."

Daisy waved him off. "I hired some guys. It's all done now."

He made a face. Now what did that expression mean? The rigid jaw, the narrowed glance. It was almost like Jamie was perturbed by the fact that she hadn't asked for his help.

She smiled to herself. God, it was so nice to have a man consider her feelings and to put her needs first. She'd never really believed there were men out there who were like that.

But apparently there were. Jamie proved it over and over again.

Squeezing his hand in pleasure, she led him inside, excited to show him how much she'd accomplished in one day of unpacking. Of course Gloria had helped, making sure everything was in the right place for "good flow" or whatever, even bringing over new cushions for the sofa and chair, giving them a face-lift.

"It's great." He gazed around. "It's so you. Your other apartment was nice. Homey. But this? This is you."

"Do you think?" She stood in the middle of the living room and turned in a slow circle. The place had a light, breezy, happy feel. "Maybe." She smiled up at him.

He touched her cheek. "How do you do it?"

"Do what?"

"Stay so…optimistic?"

She frowned, considering his words. "I don't know. Am I?"

Taking her hands, he said, "Yes. Even when you're angry." He squeezed. "You don't stay angry long. Like you always expect things to get better."

"Well, they generally do, don't they?"

He tilted his head to the side as if he wasn't sure.

"You don't agree?" She rubbed his arm. God, she loved his arms.

"My work makes me cynical."

"I get that. Your work sucks big, fat lemons, and that's speaking from experience." She gave him a playful hip check.

His face went through a transformation, from scrunched up, as if he had just sucked the very lemon Daisy spoke of, to grinning, to…something else. He leaned down to her level. "I really like you, Daisy Sinclair." He closed his eyes and took a deep breath. "And my God, you smell good."

That did it. He could tell her she was beautiful, she was smart, she was funny—those were wonderful compliments and she loved them —but for some reason, his appreciation of the way she smelled sent tingles skittering across her skin until she felt as though she glowed. Wrapping her arms around his neck, she kissed him, showing him with her lips and tongue how much she appreciated him.

As was the norm, Jamie soon took over. With his hand at the back of her head, he tilted her to the best angle for him to have her mouth. He ran his tongue along the inside of her lip before drawing her lip itself into his mouth and catching it between his teeth. His other hand dropped from the small of her back to her ass, bunching up the material of her skirt so that he could work his hand underneath.

"You need to wear skirts more."

"Why's that?" she panted.

"I like being able to feel you whenever I need to." His hand slid to the inside of her thigh, playing with the band of her panties.

"Mmm." She wriggled into his hand. "I like you being able to feel me whenever you need to."

Dipping his fingers beneath the band, he stroked her damp flesh, and a thousand-volt shock ripped through her.

"What do you say we christen this new place of yours?"

"Oh, yes." She hopped up onto the counter and wrapped her arms and bare legs around him, pressing herself into him. Taking his face in her hands, she whispered, "Christen away."

"Where? Right here?"

"For starters." She nibbled his ear, loving the tickle of

his hair on the tip of her nose. "The kitchen is the most important room in the house, after all," she whispered.

He gasped in mock shock. "That's unsanitary, Ms. Sinclair." His voice was low and sexy as he ran both hands up between her legs, moving her damp panties aside, sliding two fingers into her.

She drew in a breath. "You wouldn't want to cheat a girl out of her fantasy, would you?" Holy, it was hard to speak while Jamie was doing what he was doing.

And she loved what he was doing.

"Sex on the counter is your fantasy?" he asked, twisting three fingers inside her. And—oh!—what was he doing now? Pulsing his fingers against her inner walls?

Oh, yes. Yes, please.

Daisy threw her head back. Heaven. Absolute heaven. She'd never felt so free, so uninhibited. Never would she have shared her desire to do this with another man. But with Jamie? With Jamie she wanted to share all of her deepest, darkest secrets, everything clean and everything dirty. With Jamie she wanted nothing more than to be herself.

If he still wanted her after that?

Well, then maybe, just maybe, he was the man for—

"Jamie! Oh, Jamie!"

When had he unzipped himself? When had he slid that rubber over his length? Daisy didn't know and she didn't care. All she cared about was the fact that Jamie was inside her, filling her, holding her face between his hands and kissing her for all she was worth as he plunged in and out of her.

So perfect. So wonderful.

Her body moved with his, accepting him into her, taking his length and his width with joy and ecstasy. It was better than any damn fantasy. It was everything Daisy ever wanted.

"Oh, Daisy." Jamie groaned in her ear, his movements becoming faster, harder. "I need to come."

"Yes." She leaned back, taking more of him. "Yes. Please, Jamie, please."

He grasped her hips and hauled her against him as he thrust deep inside, his cock pulsing in release, setting off her own climax. Her body rippled with waves of pleasure that corresponded with Jamie's. Her breath in sync with his, her heart pounding in rhythm with his, she clung to him with her arms and legs, never wanting to let him go.

19

DAISY'S BED WAS like the woman herself. Soft. Inviting. Comfortable. Sexy. Delicious-smelling…

Holy. Jamie could get used to this—lying with the most beautiful woman in his arms as she lazily drew pictures on his chest, circling a couple of old bruises and tracing his tattoo. He bet if she slipped her hand a few inches lower, he'd be ready to go all over again, even though they'd already *christened* two rooms.

"You know what's weird?" she asked softly.

"Hmm?" Jamie closed his eyes, enjoying her soft caress and the sound of her voice.

"I haven't heard from my grandmother in a while."

His eyes opened. He must have misheard. "What did you say?"

"I mean, I know my grandmother's dead." Her fingers paused on his chest. "But I hear her voice in my head sometimes. Or, I used to." She resumed her drawing. "It's just memories…probably."

"What kinds of things does she say?" Jamie asked slowly.

"Oh, all kinds of things. You know? Little sayings, reminders. She reassures me when I'm down. Reminds me of important things when I'm upset or angry." Daisy laid her cheek against his chest and sighed. "It's nothing but... I miss it."

He threaded his fingers through her hair and held her against him. Because she was so loving and generous, sometimes he forgot how much she'd lost. And here she was, giving herself to him so freely when she should probably blame him for everything that had happened. She was a remarkable woman. "I don't think it matters what it is—memories, whatever. Hearing your grandmother's voice is a gift. I'm sure you'll hear from her again."

Daisy was silent for a few moments. "Jamie?"

"Yes?"

"What happened to Sarah?"

A strange chill tickled the crown of his head, spreading icy tentacles down his spine. Though his first response was to make up a story, he couldn't. After what Daisy had just revealed, Jamie needed to share something equally private. Equally important.

He just didn't know how to tell the story. Where to start.

"Was it an accident?" she asked quietly.

"No. It wasn't an accident." The words were on the tip of his tongue, but they seemed too harsh, an unfair way to sum up the demise of his sister's kind spirit, and he couldn't bring himself to say them.

"Did someone hurt her?" Daisy asked.

He had to force himself to reply. "Yes."

"They...killed her?"

He drew a deep, shuddering breath. His body went rigid. The thought of Sarah's death—her murder—still evoked the very same visceral reaction he'd felt in the first year after it happened: a hot boulder rolling around in his gut, a vise around his chest, an invisible hand around his throat.

"Oh, Jamie," she whispered. "I'm sorry." She tried to

raise her head, but he couldn't look at her right now, so he held her there, needing her close but not able to bear the sympathy in her eyes because he didn't deserve it.

"It was her boyfriend," he said finally. "We all thought he was a nice guy…" He swallowed with difficulty. "I was the last one in our family to hear from her before it happened."

"No."

Closing his eyes, Jamie tried to call forth the sound of her voice, but he couldn't, and he hated that he couldn't. "She asked for help. I didn't know it was for her, but I should have done something."

"What kind of help?"

"Information on a restraining order." His fingers tightened in Daisy's hair. "I was in my last year of law school, exam time. I rattled off the process and when she asked if she could come see me—" he squeezed his eyes shut, replaying the call for the ten millionth time "—I told her I was too busy studying."

She rubbed a thumb across his chest. After a moment of silence she said, "It wasn't your fault."

He shook his head. It was his fault. If he'd only taken the time. If he'd just listened to her, asked the right questions, he could have stopped it.

Daisy pulled herself up, elbows on his chest, gazing liquidly into his eyes. A tear stained her cheek. "It wasn't your fault."

He nodded, not because he agreed with her but simply to acknowledge he'd heard her. His head understood that, perhaps, even if he'd known what was going on, even if he'd helped Sarah, the murder-suicide might still have happened. The problem was, his heart would always wonder, would never accept what happened, and he would always blame himself.

ALL MORNING, DAISY was distracted by elements of Jamie's story from the previous night. It was so sad. Even now she found she had to sit because the idea of his sister being killed—beaten to death—by her boyfriend sucked the air right out of her lungs. The idea that Jamie blamed himself made her heart break. No wonder he was so fiercely protective. No wonder he'd wanted to help when she was down, but then pushed her away when she got too close.

She heard his voice in her head, replaying something he'd said when he'd first taken her to the gym. *Women are victims of violence way too often... They should know how to throw a punch. Where to hit. What it feels like. How not to be scared of it."*

When she'd asked whether he knew someone who'd been a victim, she hadn't given much thought to his long pause before he replied, *I think we all do.*

Wiping her cheek with the back of her hand, Daisy finished unpacking the box she'd been working on. "Jamie Forsythe is the best man I've ever met," she whispered to herself. "And I'm in love with him."

As if in reply, her phone rang, and Daisy's heart did a neat back flip in the hopes that the caller was the man himself.

"Hi, Daisy. It's Mom. Do you have a second?"

"Sure." Daisy got up and poured herself a glass of water. "Is it about the wedding?"

"No. It's about the book." There was a giddiness in her mother's voice that was not only unusual, it was infectious.

"Is it almost done?"

"No. Not my book. *Our* book."

"Our book?" Daisy shook her head, completely confused.

"The recipe book. Daisy...it's an e-book best seller!"

"What? How is that possible?"

"I don't know, but it is." She heard the sound of her mother clapping her hands through the phone. "Now they want to do a huge print run. The book is going to be in bookstores and grocery stores and Walmart and Target…" She listed off all the other places her book was going to be. "It's going to be huge!"

Daisy sat back down again. "Wow. Congratulations, Mom. You must be thrilled.""

"Thrilled? I'm over the moon! But that's not even the best part."

"What's the best part?" Wasn't the fact that the book— a tribute to her grandmother—would be available everywhere, enough?

"They're giving us an advance on the print and it's pretty generous, and with the money you raised, well, there's something Alexander and I want to propose. A venture of sorts. Can you meet us?"

JAMIE DUMPED HIS morning coffee down the sink at work. His stomach was too unsettled for coffee. Why had he told Daisy about Sarah? Why had he opened up that wound? It was too deep, too raw, too…

He clenched his fists and leaned against the counter in the staff room.

But then an image of Daisy, her cheeky smile, her rosy lips, her vulnerable and generous and sweet and exciting person, came to mind. At the thought of her, everything just seemed lighter. Better. His stomach still insisted on churning, but maybe that was more of a product of not having had a proper breakfast this morning than anything else.

He'd gone back to his place last night, explaining that all his work clothes were there, needing some space. However, once he'd returned to his apartment, it had felt even emptier than before.

"Jamie?" Helen, his assistant, called from the door. "There you are."

Jamie turned around. Was it the tone of Helen's voice or the look on her face that got his gut churning again?

"The police are on the phone."

"The police? What's going on?"

"There's been an…incident."

His flesh went cold. In his mind's eye he saw the police standing at his door, giving him the news about Sarah. In a quiet voice he asked, "What's happened?" Daisy's beautiful smile flashed before his eyes, followed quickly by a pain lancing through his skull. If something happened to Daisy…

"It's Chloe Van Der Kamp. She's been shot."

DAISY COULD BARELY contain her excitement. She'd just come from the meeting with Alexander, her mother and a real estate agent. They'd wanted to show her a place that was available for lease and to propose a joint venture. Using the money from the fundraiser and the money from the advance, plus a little capital from Alex, they wanted to help her open up a new Nana Sin's!

"I know it's a lot to take in, a lot to think about," her mother had said. "So take as much time as you need."

"What's there to think about?" Daisy had replied, taking her mother's hand. "Let's do it!"

Everything was working out for once! How could that be? Oh, who cared. All Daisy cared about was that things were looking up and she was blessed beyond reason. She had the best family, the best friends and…she was in love.

Lovely twinges raced through her veins at the thought. There was no point denying it. She was head over heels in love with Jamie Forsythe, and she wanted to share that information with him as soon as possible. Of course, he might not feel the same way, but it didn't matter.

She didn't care. She wasn't going to keep something as important as love inside anymore.

Love needed to be shared.

There was only one problem. Jamie wasn't at his place and he wasn't picking up his phone.

That left only one place for him to be. The gym.

While she waited outside on the step for someone to open the door—she really needed to talk to Jamie about giving her a key to this place—Daisy couldn't curb the nutty smile that was plastered on her face.

"Hey, Colin," she said when the door finally opened and he held it for her to enter. The fact the brothers had ever tried to pull the wool over her eyes was laughable. So she laughed.

"You're in a good mood."

"Yep." She glanced around. Some of the guys waved and called out, asking where she'd been and what she'd brought for them today. "Sorry." She held up her hands. "I'm empty-handed today. But I promise I'll be bringing more soon." Happiness exploded inside her as she thought about the future.

"If you're looking for Jamie, he's not here."

"Have you heard from him today?"

Colin shook his head. He was wearing a T-shirt and shorts. Though she'd seen him at the gym before, she'd never seen him in workout clothes. He cleared his throat. "Can I tell you something?"

"Sure. Anything."

"I want to thank you."

"For what? I haven't done anything."

"You're really good for my brother." He smiled, and Daisy decided her impression of Colin as snooty and cold had been incorrect. He was probably just one of those people who took a while to warm up.

The big doors behind her opened, and Colin craned his neck to see. "Speak of the devil. Here he is now."

Feeling as if she was composed of air and clouds—who needed the Summer Size Diet Plan when you were happy?—Daisy turned around slowly. However, the second she met Jamie's gaze, her smile dropped from her face and gravity ripped her from the clouds back down to earth.

One look at him and she knew something was terribly wrong. His menacing tone left her with no doubt.

"Daisy Sinclair? What the hell are you doing here?"

THE WORLD WAS a terrible place and no matter what Jamie did, he couldn't seem to make a difference. He couldn't seem to stop letting people down. His sister, his client… Daisy. He hadn't been able to save any of them.

The weird thing was, when he'd visited Chloe in the hospital, tubes running up her nose and machines beeping—the only indication she was still alive—it was Sarah's face he'd seen, the image of her lying in the morgue when he went to identify her, bruised and battered, almost unrecognizable from the beating that had killed her. He'd blinked the image away and suddenly it was Daisy lying in the bed, Daisy's silky curls spread out on the pillow. Daisy's body, lifeless.

The pain was excruciating.

He needed to do something about it and there was only one place to go to deal with that kind of angst. Except when he got to the gym, Daisy was there and the beast that lived inside, the one that had already been stretching its ugly head and poking his gut with its venomous claws, roared.

"What the hell are you doing here?" He strode up to her. "I told you not to come here."

Daisy wrenched her arm out of his fierce grip. "I wanted

to tell you something. A bunch of things actually. I couldn't wait so I—"

He held up his hand to stop her. It was too much. She was too much.

Too good.

Too loving.

Too trusting.

Too sweet.

He loved her too goddamn much.

"Daisy. I can't." He motioned between the two of them. "Whatever this is between us, I can't."

"What?" She blinked. "What are you talking about?"

He stared into her eyes. Cold. Bitter. Guilty. "It's over. I'm sorry."

The pain and confusion in her soft gaze only made his decision more certain. He drew himself up to his full height, crossed his arms over his chest and waited for her to leave.

She sputtered something that could have been his name, reached out to touch him, but he turned away from her hand. "I need you to leave, Daisy. Now."

"Okay," she whispered, finally. When tears started to fall from her lashes he shut his eyes, unable to watch.

"Goodbye, Jamie." He heard her pause by the door before opening it, followed by the sound of the heavy door closing behind her.

Final.

"What the hell is the matter with you?" Colin shoved him. "Why are you being such an ass?"

"You know me. I go through women like disposable razors. Isn't that what you said?" Jamie replied, his voice venomous. Rage and guilt warred so close to the surface he could taste them, rancid and sour.

"So you're just going to let the best thing that's ever happened to you walk out the door like that?"

Jamie ignored his brother's question. Blocked out the image of Daisy's stricken face. He pointed at his brother, noticing he was dressed to fight. "How's your head?"

"My head's fine. Don't deflect."

"There's no tumor?"

"No. They don't know what it is. Now, are you going to tell me what the hell is going on?"

"No. It's none of your goddamn business. Now lace up. I need to beat the living shit out of somebody."

He strode to the locker room, changed and reemerged, getting one of the guys to lace his gloves. Colin was already up there, flipping his mouth guard around in his mouth as he waited. The second Jamie climbed between the ropes, Colin came straight for him: a right jab to the jaw, followed by a left hook to his ribs. Jamie didn't bother defending himself; he wanted his brother to hit him. Needed his brother to hit him.

When Colin let up, Jamie opened his arms wide and said, "Is that all you've got?"

"There's plenty more, little brother."

Jamie blocked the first jab—out of habit—but then let his brother back him up to the ropes and go at him with a combination of blows that perfectly matched the pain in his heart.

Breathing hard, Colin said, "What the hell, Jamie?" He double-fisted him in the chest as if to wake him up. "Fight me or tell me what's going on."

"You know exactly what's going on," Jamie shouted, taking his brother by surprise with a cross to the kidneys.

Backing away, Colin used his calmly disapproving voice—the one that had driven him nuts all his life—to say, "No, actually, I don't." He followed his words with two rights and a left uppercut. Jamie blocked them all, and when his brother dropped his guard for a millisecond, Jamie took advantage, hitting him square in the jaw.

"You blame me." Jamie tried to throw another cross but Colin blocked it. That angered him. "And you should blame me."

Colin took two steps back, dropped his gloves and asked, "Blame you for what?"

"Sarah." At the mention of her name, the beast within unfurled, consuming him, taking hold of his body until he became the thing, his fists an extension of its ugly claws. His mouth giving voice to all the pain and guilt it represented. His fists flew faster than he thought possible, the power behind his punches volatile and out of control.

"Whoa, Jamie. Whoa." His brother caught him in a boxer's hug. "What the hell are you talking about?" He caught his head between his gloves. "Look at me."

It took all of Jamie's effort to focus on his brother's face, to see through the red haze that had descended over him. But eventually he did see him: the trickle of blood that ran from Colin's left nostril, the brown eyes that were clouded with concern. Clearly and slowly, Colin said, "Tell me you don't think Sarah's death was your fault."

"It was my fault," Jamie replied thickly.

Colin expelled a slow, shuddering breath. "Tell me you don't think I blame you."

"Don't you?"

His brother held his head so tightly, Jamie was unable to look away. "Christ, Jamie. Of course I don't blame you. Why would I? I blame the psychopath who killed her. That's whose fault it is. Not yours. Not mine. Not Sarah's."

20

SHE HADN'T MEANT to come back to the apartment again, but after what just happened in the gym with Jamie, Daisy felt as though she needed the comfort of her old home one last time. The only problem was her old home was unrecognizable. She'd had the place professionally cleaned and now, instead of the warm scent of yeast or cinnamon or brown sugar, all Daisy could smell was floor polish and the sour scent of all-purpose cleaner. She walked through the empty rooms—the walls had been painted, covering the dark spots where pictures had hung for years. She ran her hand across the butcher block counter top, no longer sporting the nicks and cuts from years of use because it had been sanded and refinished.

She stood in the middle of the kitchen, closed her eyes and tilted her head to the ceiling.

"One last message would be nice."

She waited. There was no dinging from the stove, no flickering of the lights…no voice in her head.

There was nothing left but silence.

With a sigh, Daisy plopped herself on the floor where her table used to be and sat cross-legged, resting her head in her hands, replaying the scene in the gym.

What on earth had just happened?

How could things have been virtually perfect between them and then have gone sideways overnight? Something had to have happened for Jamie to react like that. The question was what? Here was a man who had done everything to protect her, including putting his job on the line. He'd always been there when she needed him.

Yet now he was pushing her away? Why? Was it something she'd done?

No. Whatever it is, it wasn't you, Daisy.

The voice in her head was distinct and clear. Not her grandmother's.

Her own.

If you love him, don't let him push you away.

"You're right," Daisy said aloud, raising her head and staring at the blank wall. "You're right."

Well, there was one thing Daisy had learned, not just from living in this place with her grandmother, but in the last month with all the wonderful, crazy things that had happened. Love was the only thing that mattered. And right now, that was all she could give Jamie: her love.

Closing her eyes, she brought an image of Jamie to mind, and she drew on whatever source had given her strength over the last month and imagined sending love, pure and light, Jamie's way.

At the very least, the act made her feel better. She smiled as she thought of him, not as he'd been a half hour ago, but as he'd been last night, lying in her bed, warm and loving, protective and strong. She pictured the man who helped—anonymously—without need for thanks, who put his job on the line for others, who let others take their pain out on him—willingly. That was the Jamie she loved beyond reason.

She still had the key to his apartment, and when she was

done here, she was going to go over there and talk to him. She was going to tell him she loved him, all of him, even when he pushed her away. It was either enough, or it wasn't, but there was no way in hell she'd let him go without a fight.

It took the scream of sirens—loud and close—to rouse Daisy from her meditation. She opened her eyes. What was all that racket about? Pushing herself to her feet, she went to the window, lifted the pane and leaned out.

The overwhelming aroma of gas made her stumble back. Oh, shit.

SOMETHING BROKE IN Jamie when he heard the words, "I've never blamed you. It's not your fault." The thing inside of him released its hold on his gut and heart and left Jamie empty.

An image of Daisy's face, confused and sad, filled the hollow spaces, and Jamie smacked his head. How could he? How could he have taken out his pain and guilt on her? After everything she'd been through?

Ripping the gloves from his fists and having no time to change, Jamie grabbed his wallet and keys and sprinted from the gym. He needed to make things right with Daisy. Right now.

He loved her.

That was all there was to it.

He loved her so much it scared the hell out of him.

He needed to find her, tell her how he felt, ask for forgiveness and spend the rest of his life making it up to her. She was the best thing that had ever happened to him and he didn't deserve her, but he was going to try his hardest to earn it.

Revving the engine on the bike, he made a U-turn in the middle of the street and took off to her place. Except that he wasn't going to her new place. He headed to the old building. Jamie didn't know why. He just felt very strongly that Daisy would be there.

Two blocks away, however, he had to pull over because the street was blocked. Fire trucks, police cars, barricades blocked the way. Jamie pushed the bike as close as possible, his heart racing, a feeling of dread filling his lungs. He parked, climbed off and attempted to slip past the roadblock.

"Sorry, sir. You've got to stay behind the barricades," a young police officer informed him.

"My girlfriend's place is in there. I need to make sure she's all right. Please." Jamie craned his neck, trying to see past the flashing lights and vehicles as fear stampeded through his veins. "What's going on?" The officer turned away, so Jamie called louder. "Someone tell me what's going on."

"It's a gas leak."

Jamie turned. The woman of his dreams was staring up at him with a quirky smile lighting her rosy cheeks.

"Daisy!" He picked her up and spun her around. "Oh my God, Daisy! You're okay. Oh, thank God you're okay."

She wrapped her arms around him. "So…who's this girlfriend you were talking about?"

He set her down and stared into her sparkling eyes, running his fingers through her hair to the back of her head, bringing her close. He leaned down and whispered, "You. If you'll have me."

"Hmm," she hummed playfully. "I'll consider it."

Resting his forehead against hers, he whispered, "I'm so sorry. I didn't mean any of that stuff I said."

She pulled back. "Then why'd you say it?"

He touched her jaw, his eyes focusing on her lips. "Something happened to one of my clients. She was hurt and I felt…responsible. I took it out on you." He rubbed her cheek. "It was so stupid. I'm so stupid. Will you forgive me?"

She rubbed his chest, making gentle circles with her small hands. "You know, I may have said a lot of things I didn't mean when I was upset, too. Like... I hate you and I never want to see you again...you know, little things like that." She twisted her lips. "When probably all along I was really falling in love with you."

"Daisy." His mouth found hers, parted already for him, the sweet taste of forgiveness on her lips, the delicious flavor of love on her tongue.

"I'll forgive you if you forgive me," she whispered.

"There's nothing to forgive."

"Good. Then it's all settled." She pulled back, her sparkling eyes lighting up with an ethereal glow that was the most beautiful thing he'd ever seen. "Now, want to come see what I've been up to?"

DAISY HELD ON TO Jamie as he drove his bike through the streets of Chicago's warehouse district and parked in front of a large building with a for-lease sign in the window. She climbed off the back, marveling at how much better she was getting at climbing on and off of the thing, even when wearing a dress.

From her bag, she took out the key she'd just been given by her new partners and opened the front door. The front of the building was her favorite part. "This is it," she said with a grin. "This is the new home of Nana Sin's."

"What?" Jamie grinned wide. "Really?"

"Yep. Would you like a tour?"

"Of course."

"This front area is three times larger than the last one, lots of room for people to sit and shelves for all the stuff. In addition to the baked goods, we're going to sell cookbooks and other Nana Sin paraphernalia—T-shirts, coffee cups, gift baskets, that sort of thing."

"Good idea."

She took him to the back, where the kitchen was. "This space needs renovating, but if we do it right, it'll give us twice as much room as my old kitchen. You know what that means?"

Jamie took her hand and squeezed. "You can produce twice as much?"

"Exactly. Maybe more. I can hire more people, do more things. We'll create an online ordering system, maybe do some corporate catering. I don't know, but the possibilities are endless."

"So, who is this 'we' you keep mentioning?"

"My mother and Alex. They're going to invest and help with business planning. They have some really good ideas and… I think we'll work well together." Daisy looked around. She didn't see the dusty, rundown space as it was now; she saw it for what it would become; an efficient kitchen full of people and mouthwatering goods. Her vision also included a new and close relationship with her mother.

"That's wonderful." Jamie beamed down at her, and Daisy suddenly realized he had a bruise blooming high on his right cheekbone. She reached tentatively to touch it. "What happened?"

"Colin." He touched his face and winced. "He hit me until I saw the light."

"And what light is that?"

Wrapping his arms around her, he said, "That I'm an idiot and that I love you."

She smacked his chest. "I knew it!"

God, she loved the sound of his laugh. Still smiling, he framed her face, not saying anything until his expression turned serious. "I don't want to lose you."

She helped herself to his belt loops, yanking him close. "Good. I don't want to be lost."

As if he didn't hear her, he continued, "I want you in my life. For good."

"Good. I want to be in your life. For good." She slid one hand up his abdomen.

"I don't remember what I did without you." His hands sifted through her hair.

"Good." She undid a button on his shirt and then a second. "Because I've got all kinds of plans about what you're going to do to me now. And we're going to start right here in the kitchen." She hopped up on the dusty counter.

"What is it about you and kitchen counters?" He cupped her jaw, drawing his thumb across her lips.

"Don't know, but they make me hot." She finished the buttons on his shirt.

"I'm shocked, Daisy. Sex in an industrial kitchen has *health and safety violation* written all over it."

From somewhere in the ether, Daisy swore she heard her grandmother's hearty chuckle echoing between the industrial pipes in the rafters. Pointing her face to the ceiling, she whispered, "I knew you'd come back!"

"What did you say?"

"Nothing." She grinned, happier than she had ever been before. "Now, shut up and kiss me."

* * * * *

Love a really sexy story?
Watch for Daire St. Denis's next book,
BIG SKY SEDUCTION,
coming May 2016,
only from Harlequin Blaze!